LEVON'S SCOURGE

A VIGILANTE JUSTICE THRILLER, BOOK
TWELVE

CHUCK DIXON

ROUGH
EDGES
PRESS

LEVON'S SCOURGE

BOOK I

MEXICO

1

Gunny Leffertz said:
"The more you kill distant, the less you kill close."

Idaho

THERE WERE four of them that came by night.

They parked the stolen Bronco in a copse of pines out of sight of the road. From there they hiked overland to the west. Once over a ridge, they turned south. The house and surrounding buildings would be just past the skeletal figures of leafless dogwoods that lay in a line before them. They could see the glow of pole lights beneath a lowering sky of iron-colored clouds. It would snow soon. They wanted the job done and over before the first flake fell. They did not like the cold. They did not like this place. It had to be tonight.

Keeping to the shadows beneath a fringe of larch and spruce, they followed a post and rail fence around to a stable building. From the shelter of a hay crib, they surveyed the property. A ranch-style house sat at the back of a broad stable yard. There was a carport with a single vehicle parked inside. A travel trailer was the only other habitable structure.

There were lights on somewhere in the interior of the house. The stuttering blue glow of a television set was cast against the windows of one of the rooms. This was the only sign of life. All was quiet as expected at three in the morning. The only sound was the rustle of wind through the grass.

The leader of the four hissed and gestured to the others. One would come with him. The other two would separate to check the stable and the trailer.

The leader and his second approached, rifles raised, aimed at the windows and door of the house. The others moved at a trot toward the stable and trailer.

Twenty yards from the house. Ten yards from the house. All remained dark outside the pools of light from the two pole lamps by the stable and along the paddock fence. No motion detection lamps lit up.

At the door, the leader crouched to work a short pry bar into the door jamb by the deadbolt. His second stood braced on the walk, his rifle trained to the door. A couple of pulls and the bolt came free, and they were inside the house moving swiftly into the dark interior.

Outside, one of the men crept to the door of the trailer. He winced as the aluminum step creaked under the weight of his boot. The screen door was unlatched, and he pulled it open with caution before trying the exterior door. This was unlocked and he turned the knob and, stooping low, used the end of his barrel to lever it open. The inside had the dead smell of an unoccupied place. The musk of old grease and the dry scent of dust. No one had lived here for a month or more.

Inside the stables, the other man found the stalls empty. A musty odor of rotten straw hung in the air. The shelves of the tack room were bare. Saddle racks sat empty. He turned to step outside where the other was moving in the shadow cast by the trailer. They each took positions, as they had been ordered, to remain outside to watch the house. They would move in if called or if they saw any movement that was not one of their own.

The man by the trailer set his rifle down atop a picnic table. He removed woolen gloves to rub his numbed hands together. He cupped them before his mouth to blow warm air onto them. He'd never felt cold like this. Not even the time he worked in the reefer house at the shrimp packer. This was a different cold. A man could die from this cold.

He heard a sharp sound. A cough. It was like the bark of a kit fox. It made him look up. He could no longer see the man by the stables. He searched around until he saw a humped figure lying still on the ground. He stepped from the shadows with his rifle raised.

The fox barked once more, though he never heard it.

Within the house, the leader and his second moved with practiced ease, one behind the other with rifles pressed to their shoulders and eyes trained ahead. The rooms were empty and gave the impression of long disuse. The place was unheated. They could see their breath as they moved through. The furniture remained but the usual detritus of everyday life was missing. Bookshelves were empty. In the kitchen all but the large appliances were gone. Cabinets lay empty and open. Only a single plate and coffee mug in the sink showed signs of recent habitation.

The muffled sound of a television came from behind a door off the kitchen. The strobing glow of the set was visible through the gap beneath the door. The rising and falling of dramatic music sounded tinny through the door.

The leader gestured for his second to try the door. The second crouched low, rifle hanging in its sling, his fist tight on the pistol grip, as he turned the knob. The leader stood close behind, rifle raised. The second pushed the door in with steady pressure, the black snout of his weapon poking before him. The door was halfway open, the full volume of the TV reaching them. Sounds of gunfire and neighing horses. A cowboy movie.

A sudden peal of thunder drowned out all sound. The leader was pitched backward by a blunt force striking his chest armor. His ears rang and he fought for breath where he'd fallen to the floor. He raised himself up despite the agony he felt across his sternum and ribs. He emptied half a magazine into the room. The sound and glow of the television ended abruptly leaving him in smoke-filled gloom.

The leader struggled to his knees, the rifle trained into the dark of the room. The second lay inside the doorframe. His head, and torso above the shoulders, were gone. With rising gorge, the leader realized that his own face, chest, and arms were sticky with the remains of his second.

He fired the rest of the magazine through the walls around the doorway. He rolled aside to switch out magazines before rising to his feet. The rifle held at his hip, he moved toward the dark opening. With the light of a pencil torch, he scanned the interior.

It was a laundry room. A flat-screen TV hung dark now on a rear wall. A clothes washer had been pulled from its place by a dryer to sit sideways to the doorway. Bolted down atop the washer was a double-barrel shotgun with a cable slung from the trigger to the inside knob of the door. His second had caught most of both barrels. A few stray balls had struck the leader in his armor.

He pressed his back to an exterior wall to tab at the handheld on his belt.

There was no answering squawk.

He tabbed again.

No answer.

With an animal snarl, he rushed to the open front door and into the stable yard. Two figures lay still, black against the dark ground. He turned then in time to feel a hammer blow against his shoulder. The rifle fell from his hand, his grip gone, fingers nerveless. A sudden weakness caused him to drop to one knee. A second blow struck him in the side to spill him to the earth.

He lay, feeling a warm sensation spreading over his flesh. It was his own blood. Vapor rose from beneath the body armor, his life escaping into the night chill. Unable to move, he lay on his side looking out at the gray clouds hanging so low he might touch them.

Snow was falling now. Tiny flakes fell through the dry air. It would be a heavy fall lasting days.

LEVON REMOVED his eye from the cup of the scope and set aside the heavy Model 70.

He picked up the pump shotgun that lay by him in his hide to make his way from under the low boughs of the scotch pine that had been his home for the past week.

He was satisfied that the last of them were dead but would take no chances. He walked down the shallow slope at the back of the house to move toward the still figure lying halfway to the trailer. Eyes over the front bead of the shotgun, he neared the man. A lake of blood dusted with fresh snow turned pink spread beneath the man. Near all the blood he had.

The first 30-06 round was a failed headshot that had

taken the man in the shoulder. Though it failed to pierce the armor it caused the man to turn side on where Levon's next round took him in the seam of the vest where the armor was thinnest. A kill shot to the thorax.

Levon kicked the tricked-out M4 away from the man's palsied hand. With a toe of his work boot he flipped the man on his back and crouched to examine his features. The man's hard features were melted into an appearance of childlike wonder, eyes wide and jaw slack. A neck tattoo of a coiled snake made a lie of that innocent expression.

He stood then to approach the other two corpses that lay in the stable yard. Both taken in head shots. This did not please him as much as to reassure him that he had not lost his eye. Levon took no joy in killing. In fact, he felt nothing when he took another man's life. He realized that this should trouble him. But that was something to be dealt with on another day in another place.

For now, there was only the work to be done.

2

Gunny Leffertz said:

"Intel. Intel. Intel. Beg, borrow, or steal to get it. But get it."

Nashville

THE ONLY THING better than an under-par round of golf was a good day at the gun range.

And it had been a damned good day in more ways than one for Randall "Duck" Withers.

"And that, gentlemen, is how it's done," Randall said, raising the barrel of the Henry rifle from the bench rest. He punched the return button and the silhouette target sped along the cable back toward him.

Randall held the target up to them. Eight holes in the center of the cartoon gunfighter's Stetson. Two more in the chest. The half dozen Chinese gentlemen bowed and nodded; smiles fixed on their faces. The ear protectors, yellow-tinted safety glasses and orange plastic vests over their business suits made them look like extras in a cheap science fiction movie. But these guys collected worth was north of two hundred billion bucks so Randy kept his smartass remarks to himself.

"Now, who's gonna give it a try?" he said, holding out the rifle after refilling the tube magazine with long Colts.

The CEO of Tri-Tech was first to step forward and Randall helped him with some advice on holding the butt firm to his shoulder and squeezing rather than jerking the trigger. These Orientals had requested to fire western heritage guns and Randall obliged with a selection of six-shooters and lever actions. They all wanted to be Clint Eastwood for a day and the customer was always right.

He'd done some of the best shooting of his life treating some clients to an afternoon at Thunder Mountain outside Nashville. He really impressed the hell out of the gaggle of Taiwanese business owners with some rifle and handgun shots that surprised even him. Withers had always been a good shot, scoring high in his Ranger unit for marksmanship at Bragg once he got over his noise aversion problems, but today it was like God was guiding his aim.

It all served to close the deal with the Taipei import company looking to provide security for its execs traveling overseas. What with Xi on the mainland flexing his muscles and Taiwan feeling the heat, these high rollers wanted to make sure they were safe from Beijing's dirty tricksters as well as their own homegrown Society of the Continent troublemakers. And it was looking like Bryson Tactical Services was going to nail that fat contract.

After an amazing day of sharpshooting for him and a loud, if piss-poor, performance by his clients, they parted company with the promise to meet for dinner at Morton's.

Randall drove his rented Escalade to the Loews Vanderbilt where he looked forward to a hot needle shower followed by an ice-cold V&T. After dinner tonight, the contract locked up over lobster and rib eyes, he'd put his customers to bed and check out the talent down at the hotel bar.

At the lobby of the hotel, he was summoned over to the registration desk. The chirpy girl behind the counter handed him a FedEx box addressed to him.

"This came while you were out, sir," she said, showing every tooth in her head with a forced professional glee.

"Okay," he said, scanning the waybill. It was an overnight a.m. delivery. A return address in Colorado from an MF Ltd.

Up in his room, he tossed the package on his bed and stripped to take a shower. Refreshed, the sulfur stink of the range off him, he slipped into a plush robe and padded to the mini-bar where he built a tall drink from a toy-sized bottle of Stoli and half bottle of Schweppes over a tower of ice. He lounged back against pillows and flipped on the flatscreen to zip through the channels until he found a hockey game out of Calgary.

Two long pulls on the V&T and he grabbed up the package to pull the tab free. The only contents were a phone and a Post-it note. The phone was a new, off-brand smartphone, fully charged. Stuck to the screen, the Post-it read: CALL ME WHEN YOU GET THIS.

"Shit," Randall said, the vodka turning bitter on his tongue.

———

"YOU TOLD me you'd never reach out to me again, Levon."

"Yeah."

"It was a promise."

"And I meant it, Duck."

"So, you gonna bullshit me that *this* last time is the *real* last time?"

"I wouldn't be doing this if I didn't have to."

"Who'd you fuck with this time?"

"Someone who won't give up on me. My family too."

"Shit, Levon."

"I sent them away. Even I don't know where they are."

"So, what can I do?"

"I need to know who's on me. I sent you some pictures."

"I'll have a look. Not sure what I can do."

"You have the connections through your business, Duck. Law enforcement and private security all over. Someone will know who these assholes were."

"Like I said, I'll look them over and call you back."

"That's all I ask."

"Till next time, your jarhead motherfucker."

There were more than a dozen photos in the gallery on the phone.

Four men stripped naked and lying in the snow. Dead men. One headless. Two more nearly so. Fresh kills. Cade did not play.

Each of their graying hides was covered in tattoos. Whole sleeves, chests, and backs. Some denser and more extensive than others. The usual snakes, skulls, dice, aces of spades, guns, naked senoritas. There were close-ups showing details of the ink. One of them, the only one with an intact skull, bore an impressively fierce Michael the Archangel across his chest, spread wings and flaming sword and everything. Above the angel was an ornately lettered scroll that read: *Real Hasta La Muerte*. Ride or Die.

It could have been any of a half dozen cartels but for a distinctive squiggle design inked on the calf of one corpse and the wrist of another. On each was *Libertate Unanimus* in cursive letters.

There were also two photos of an older Ford Bronco. A

full shot of the two-tone SUV in red and white and a detail shot of the license plate. Texas.

"What the actual fuck," Randall said to himself, seated on the corner of the bed.

▭

"EVER HEAR of The Perfect Ten Soldiers?" Randall asked as he walked across the lobby of the Loews Vanderbilt.

"That's a new one on me," Levon said in his earbud.

"They're freelance hunter killers out of Curaçao."

"Where?"

"It's a Dutch Colony off the coast of Venezuela," Randall said as he handed his ticket to the parking valet. "Tiny little place. Poor as shit. Great beaches."

"So, there's only six now."

"That's not how it works, dumbass," Randall said as he waited along the curb. "'Perfect Ten' refers to the quality of their work. I've got no goddamn clue how many of the little fuckers there are."

"They hire out."

"And they're not cheap."

"Looks like a dead end."

"Unless you follow any cookie crumbs they left behind."

"Did those plates check out?"

"Yeah. Stolen Wednesday last week."

"Where?"

"Webb County."

"That's Laredo, isn't it?"

"Sure is. That help you any, Levon?"

"Starting to add up. I have a few leads. Thin ones. I'll prod until they break cover."

"It's what you do, Levon. Keep tugging that string." Randall watched his Escalade pulling up from the valet lot.

"This is the last time, Duck. I promise." The earbud hissed and the call ended.

"Till next time," Randall said, handing off a twenty to the valet.

On the way to his dinner meeting at Morton's, he tossed the burner phone from the car somewhere along Route 40.

3

San Antonio

VAPOR ROSE off the brown water of the river in the predawn chill. It was more of a canal really, snaking through the heart of the city. A paved walk ran along either of the raised banks past municipal buildings, historic sites and clutches of shops and restaurants. The Riverwalk drew more tourists than the mission at the Alamo, which it ran past. In these early morning hours before the out-of-towners showed up in droves, it was occupied by runners, joggers and the occasional bike.

Levon felt he was starting to get his wind back as he loped easy in the cool-down phase of his run. The T-shirt under his hoodie was plastered to him after ten miles. But he felt good and looked forward to a stretch and long soak in the tub.

Always active in one way or another, he'd been neglecting his cardio since arriving at the ranch up in Idaho. It showed in his breath control. That last man at the ranch should never have taken two shots. Since showing up in Texas he started his daily runs again, working up from five miles to now fifteen inside of two weeks. The bridges over the river allowed him to make loops back to his starting point. And he was able to make the loop a little longer with each run.

Each day he pushed the wall of pain further back. Each day ended with him feeling sore but stronger. It got so he looked forward to waking up to these runs and that was the best sign of all. Yes, the runs hurt more than they once did, and he was a few seconds longer getting back to his resting heart rate. But that was age and there wasn't a damned thing he could do about that.

Other than building endurance and wind, the runs allowed his mind to go into a near trance. These hours spent running were the only time he allowed his concentration to stray off mission. His thoughts always went to Merry and Hope and he wondered how they were doing. He was sure his uncle Fern had taken them far from Idaho. That old badger knew how to hide and had a network of old friends that would prove impossible to trace. Old friends and getting older. The Marines of Fern Cade's time in service were starting to die off. Fewer every year.

Levon put from his mind the day when he would see his girls again. They had a pre-arranged signal that would let them know all was clear and that their father was coming home. But he knew there was no certainty that the day would ever come. It might just be that he would have to stay away from them forever, spend a lifetime running. Another possibility is that he might die in his efforts to get them all shed of the men who were stalking him.

San Antonio proved to be a good place to hide himself while he worked out a strategy. He'd never been here before so there was little chance he'd run into anyone he knew. And with a population rapidly growing to a million and a half, the city had lost its small-town feel. Transplants from California and other places were moving to the state to escape crime and high taxes. While that probably didn't make the natives very happy, it provided the anonymity that Levon required.

He slowed to a walk at the 9th Street Bridge and crossed over to follow the street to where he'd left his car parked in a garage. He chose an older building that had no security camera at the pay booth. The eight-year-old Toyota Sequoia he'd bought with cash under the name Arthur Stone was on the second level where he left it. He popped the back and rested against the tailgate to drain a bottle of water. He opened a second bottle to sip as he drove to the no-star motel off 281 where he'd taken a room for the week. As he drove through the early morning gray, his mind returned to the mission.

There was little to go on. He knew now that the men who came to the ranch were specialists. They were killers. And they probably came at a high price. Whoever sent them would send more when they eventually realized their hired guns were never coming back. It might be summer by the time the bodies of the four tattooed men were found in a dry wash west of the ranch. By then they would be picked near clean by coyotes and turkey vultures. And what the animals didn't consume the elements and the ants would.

Their employers would know the men had failed long before that when the gunmen did not return to ask for the balance of their fee. That meant another team would be found, a more skilled group of men, and sent out to kill him.

Chances were, they were already sniffing along his back trail.

He considered setting up another snare for the new players. Maybe this time capture one alive to get further intel. That could prove to be a wash, he reckoned. Whoever wanted him would keep several degrees of separation from themselves and their mercenary hires.

So, who was it that was after him?

His last encounter with a cartel ended in what he considered a draw. That wasn't to say that there was unquestionable honor in the men of the Sinaloa and the Zetas. Some hot-shit *sicario* from one of the *plazas* could get in his head to make a name for himself by taking out a troublemaking *gabacho*. Only there was nothing here that meshed with that theory. A *cabrone* looking to make a name for himself would want to be the one to pull the trigger himself, not hire outside talent to do the job. And for damned sure not bring on non-Mexicans to do the work. That kind of deal would not inspire *corridos* to be written.

As Levon made the on-ramp up onto the highway, he ran down the list of other high rollers he'd pissed off.

He'd stirred an anthill back in Alabama and Georgia by ripping a new one in that cabal of child traffickers. In addition to a houseful of corpses, he left a few powerful men with their careers in tatters. That included a sitting congressman who decided to put a bullet in his own brain. The rest had run for the cover of lawyers or dug deep into their favor banks to stay out of the limelight or a prison cell. An incurious media and a deeply corrupted system aided them in this. But that didn't mean they didn't still have raw feelings about the man who broke up their sick enterprise.

The reappearance of Lew Dollinger in his life was proof of that. But the ex-cop made assurances that it wasn't his former masters who'd set him on Levon's scent. For reasons of his own, Dollinger had shared all he had on the men who'd assigned him to find Levon Cade. It wasn't much. A credit card paid for by a shell company registered in Nevada. A few phone calls confirmed that Zentropic LLC was nothing more than a post box in Reno.

There was also Dollinger's description of the man who'd hired him. A slender Asian man that Dollinger said sounded "more like a snooty Englishman than your average gook." That pointed to an international organization. Something bigger than a domestic sex ring or more foreign than a Mexican cartel.

It had to link back to what happened to him in Maine. To the men he killed there at Lake Bellevue. The money and gems and files he'd found in the vault of one of the billionaire's mansions. Whoever was after him would know that he'd traded much of the cash and all of the intel to the feds in exchange for amnesty. Perhaps it was someone at one of the agencies who leaked his real identity to the men who now wanted him dead. Maybe it was some of the dirty cash he'd spent from the hoard he'd found in Corey Blanco's vault. Or it could have been as simple as him co-signing that business loan for Fern's distillery back in 'Bama. Somehow, he'd stepped into the clear long enough for them to get a bead on him.

It was only by God's good mercy that he'd uprooted himself and the girls to vanish west when they did. It might just have been the hunter/killers out of Curaçao could have shown up in his holler and caught him unawares. They would not have spared Merry and Holly in their vengeance. He'd seen evidence enough of the sort of animals these men employed. He'd run forever to draw them away from his daughters.

Or willingly die knowing the trail would go cold with him.

He pulled into the lot of the Motel 8 and found a slot a few doors down from the metal steps that led to his room on the second tier. Inside the room, he stripped and ran a steaming shower. Stepping from the shower, he closed the drain to allow it to fill with water. Padding naked into the main room he pulled an ice-cold protein drink from the mini-fridge. It was one he'd prepared himself in a blender before taking off for his run. He sipped it while preparing a two-cup pot of coffee in the little maker provided. The tub near full, he returned to the bathroom and slipped into the steaming water to continue sipping the protein shake from the plastic blender bottle.

Setting the empty bottle aside on the bathmat, he rested his head on a towel folded behind his neck. He let the warm water leech the ache from his legs and back while his mind returned to the mission.

Another strategy he considered was trying to find Lew Dollinger. If Levon could locate him, the man might be useful as a stalking horse. After all, the men hunting Levon would also be trying to find Dollinger. The wily old fox had betrayed them to Levon and disappeared himself. It would be hard to uncover him but not impossible.

In the end, Levon decided against it. Dollinger might be an odious bottom feeder but he'd possessed just enough honor to alert Levon of the danger his family was in. That would make it wrong on Levon's part to use the man as bait. At least for now.

Though, should time and circumstances warrant it, he would stake the albino cracker out like a fatted calf.

Levon had other avenues to explore, other folks who owed him for favors past. He'd call them all in now.

He had to.

It was about his girls now.

4

Gunny Leffertz said:
"How you hide depends on who's looking for you."

Anchorage

YOU CAN'T RUN FOREVER. Any fool knew that.

It was only a matter of time, weeks, months, before the skinny little gook and his bulls caught up with him. Given that, Lew Dollinger was going to give them one hell of a run.

He was more than a week past the two-week grace period the Asian fella in the dago cut suit had given him. He drove his piece-of-shit Tundra all the way west to Stockton, California. With keys still in the ignition and the doors unlocked, he parked it near a Trailways terminal where he paid cash for a round trip to San Francisco.

Once in Babylon-by-the-Bay he stopped into a Wells Fargo bank to make a cash withdrawal of twenty thousand dollars using the Centurion Card the gook had given him to cover expenses. He was a little surprised they hadn't canceled it on him. But then, this was their only current tether to him. Using it would send the balloon up. They'd know, for the first time in weeks, where Lew was. The chase was on for real now.

His next stop was a Ralph's where he bought a thousand dollars' worth of twenty-five-dollar Amazon gift cards. He handed these out in the parking lot to any and all comers. They were gone inside of a minute. That was forty blind alleys for the gook to chase down. Forty-one if they thought he might use the return on that round-trip ticket back to Stockton. It all might buy him a day or two. That's all the time he'd need.

Paying cash again, he took another Trailways north to Seattle and booked passage on a cruise ship making a two-week trip along the coast of Alaska. He used his last hold-out fake ID under the unimaginatively named Robert Williams. Once on the ship, he was safe at home as long as the boat stayed at sea. It was as far as he could get without a passport. Two weeks was enough time to figure out his next move. He had enough reserve cash for a new identity that would allow him out of the country.

Outfoxing the little gook and his goons might even have been fun if Lew didn't think about how ugly it could end for him. These boys, whoever they were, played rough. But Lew's motto was "live for the day." At least since he made the bonehead decision to let Levon Cade in on the game. It was a moment of weakness on his part that he couldn't quite explain to himself. Maybe it was because Cade spared his life back in Alabama. Maybe it was him feeling sorry for Cade or fearful of what might happen to Cade's little girls if the skinny Asian prick caught up with them. Maybe it just galled him to let that yellow bastard win and Lew playing a part in it like some whipped coon hound.

Dollinger thought that Cade might have had this same sort of quandary that night when he let Lew walk away. Now that moment of mercy had paid off for Cade. The man he spared, Lew himself, turning into a kind of guardian angel for him. Might be, Lew hoped, that fate, karma, or the baby Jesus himself, would repay his own kindness in much the same way. Though he'd little promise of that. Lew knew the kind of sinner he was. He knew full well that one good deed wasn't going to save his ass in the end. Not with the tally of sins he'd racked up in his forty-plus years. No divine intervention was going to spare him from whatever might fall upon his head once the little gook caught him up.

He only hoped it'd be quick when it ended.

For now, he was well out to sea, snug in his little interior cabin. Though, he didn't spend much time in its cramped quarters. A boat like this was full up of single pussy. Sure, a bit longer in the tooth than he'd like. Widows and retired teachers and gaggles of middle-aged gal pals out on a toot around the Yukon. Even a dog-faced specimen like Lew could find a partner for slap and tickle with the four-to-one ratio of females to males on this bon voyage. Especially when the men on board averaged sixty and over.

A day out of Sitka he managed to sidle up to a choice piece of rump along the rails of C deck during a whale watching session. Her name was Kathleen Griggs, on sabbatical from Iowa State, and, even bundled up in a parka and woolen pants, he could tell she had the sort of curves he liked on a woman. She had a sweet smile and there were only a few streaks of gray in the yellow bangs that poked from under her knit toque.

As an opener, Lew made an off-color remark about the

sex life of blue whales and was rewarded with a chuckle. That told him she was a sport and so he cranked up the good old boy charm. The next thing he knew they were sharing dinner together and then the bunk in her more spacious starboard facing cabin on an upper deck.

She believed him to be a retired policeman who'd been recently widowed and traveling on a budget to forget his loss. Well, half of that was almost true. He'd been police but never dumb enough to marry. He was "Bobby" to her, and he called her "Kat." She was an educated woman and ignorant of the world as only the truly educated can be. He figured she viewed him like someone would a zoo animal, an unreconstructed brute as far from her world of seminars and classes as would be some African hottentot. He told her lies that contained enough truth to help him remember them. She ate them up like a kid hearing bedtime stories or a sailor listening to a dirty joke.

It all served to take his thoughts away from being the object of a manhunt. Even if it was for the duration of a sit-down meal or a slow screw in her cabin. At least while they were on the water, he was safe.

When they docked the third morning at Anchorage for a two-day stop, he managed to slip off board without Kat's company. He left her a note that he'd meet her at the Haute Quarter Grill for lunch. It was a place some school teacher friends of hers told her she *had* to visit if she was ever up this way.

Lew made his way down to the galley deck and joined a few crewmembers exiting onto the pier through a sally port. Through the bitter cold, he crunched over snow-dusted asphalt to a cab stand where a row of salt-stained taxis stood waiting. He boarded a Chevy Blazer with a once-colorful Yukon Cab wrap over its rusting body.

He reached over the back seat and dropped a twenty next to the driver.

"I'm lookin' for a strip club," he said.

"Like a gentlemen's club or..." the Inuit driver began turning to reveal a gap-toothed smile.

"A shithole," Lew interrupted. "Cheap beer and cheaper pussy."

"You got it, friend," the driver said and put the cab in gear.

The place was called Tail Feathers and sat at the end of a row of steel buildings in what looked like an industrial park. The only distinguishing feature was the club's name in two-foot-high Day-Glo letters painted on the wall by a hot pink silhouette of a big-titted chick lounging on her ass with her back arched. Lots of four-wheel pickups were pulled up out front. Real war machines with fat tires and lift kits.

This was the place.

"You done here, give me a call and I take you back dock-side," the Inuit said, exchanging a business card for the twelve-dollar fare and five-dollar tip.

The bar's interior was as unimpressive as the outside. All was kept dim but for the baby spots illuminating two girls languidly tramping around a raised stage at the center of an oval bar. The darkness hid the hangar-like environment from view. Though the corrugated walls weren't helping the acoustics any. A Tom Petty song was echoing tinny as the naked babes on the runway dipped and wiggled in something like synchronization to the beat.

Men sat at the bar and in Naugahyde upholstered booths knocking back tallboys to wash down baskets of cheese fries. They seemed indifferent to the working girls, and it was no wonder. This was the day shift, and the swirl of tinted party lights did little to hide stretch marks and cellulite.

Lew took a stool at a corner of the bar and ordered a double Maker's Mark and a tumbler of ice. The pencil-neck bartender brought his drink and Lew laid down a fifty.

"Your boss in?" Lew said, putting his hand atop the fingers that reached out of the bill.

"Nicolai!" the bartender called toward the blackness at the back of the place.

A Russian, Lew thought with a dry smile. It was always a Russian.

Gunny Leffertz said:

"Spilled blood will bind men to each other. Even someone else's blood."

Coatzacoalcos

THE HOUSE SAT WELL BACK off a broad beach. The morning sun flashed golden off the lazy gulf waves that licked the shore.

Levon followed a trail worn in the sand that ran alongside a length of dune fence. A set of wooden steps, bleached gray by time, led up to a walkway of crumbling asphalt. The house lay beyond it, visible over the swaying tops of marram grass. A sprawling ranchero with roof tiles frosted white by salt scour. Chains squeaked in a rusting swing set that sat sagging behind a walled courtyard running across the back of the house. A soccer goal made of PVC piping. The torn netting shifted in the wind off the water. Sharp shards of glass sparkled like diamonds where they were embedded in the concrete atop the wall.

The lenses of cameras set under the eaves flashed in the rising sun. Levon stopped before one to allow it to see him. He held his hands open at his sides. He lifted his T-shirt to show his tanned belly and turned to show his bare back and empty waistband. He followed the courtyard around to the front of the house where a wrought-iron fence enclosed the front yard. It was more defensive than decorative with triangular spikes atop it to discourage climbers. The fence was taller than Levon and set in a cinder block knee wall.

He waited at the gate until he heard the lock buzz. He worked the latch and stepped onto the pebble walkway that led to the inset front door of the house. One of the double doors opened and a man stepped into the shade of a narrow entryway. The man was brown as teak and wore drawstring pants with a guayabera shirt open over a bare muscular chest.

"Yayo," Levon said as he approached.

"I'm torn, *amigo*," the man said, stepping into the sunlight. "It pleases me to see you even though I'd hoped never to see you again."

"My apologies for that," Levon said in unaccented Spanish as he took the other man's offered hand. "I wish I could say this was strictly a social visit."

"And here I was looking forward to another unexciting day by the sea." The man grinned and clapped a hand on Levon's shoulder to usher him inside. He was a good head or more shorter than Levon but powerfully built.

"I'm just here for talk," Levon said.

"Then we'll talk," the man said.

Levon followed the other man through the cool dark interior of the house. Music played somewhere and he heard children's voices calling to one another. They moved into a sunny kitchen that sat at the back of the house. A woman was busy at a marble-topped island chopping vegetables. An Indio with large eyes set in gamine features. She might have been pretty if she wasn't offering the visiting gringo a deep scowl as greeting. The man patted the air in her direction to assure her that their guest was a trusted friend. Her expression softened somewhat but the disapproval was still there in her dark eyes.

They sat in chairs on a broad veranda shaded by an awning. This level was raised above the courtyard offering a view of the Gulf over the dunes.

Eduardo Lugo settled in his chair and eyed Levon with a wry smile.

"I always called you Tomas," he said. "That was never your name, was it?"

"It was a mask," Levon said, sitting forward in his chair, hands clasped together, eyes on the golden sea. "Like the one you wore."

"Such a life that we cannot even let our friends know our names or see our faces," the other man sighed. "You are no longer military?"

"No. And you left *los marinos?*"

"I resigned my commission seven years ago. I teach school now. No one here knows of my past. It's better that way."

"Was it that trouble in Tamaulipas?"

"You heard of this?" Eduardo raised an eyebrow.

"I keep up."

Eduardo "Yayo" Lugo had been a captain in Mexico's Marines, their naval infantry. Los Marinos was the only entirely uncorrupted entity in the country and, aside from the American DEA, the most effective deterrent to the drug trade. They often collaborated with American law enforcement agencies on raids and interdictions. It was los Marinos who busted "Chapo" Guzman the final time, the time that ultimately led to his incarceration in the United States. Over time, the gringo lawmen became disenchanted with the Mexican marines' often more direct approach to the war on drugs.

The full effectiveness of the marines came to an end with the disappearance of thirty cartel members arrested in the state of Tamaulipas in the northeastern portion of Mexico. The Mexican press, largely influenced and even owned by the cartels, turned against the marines. The DEA and FBI stepped away from their longtime relationship with the now radioactive corps. Once heroes, men like Yayo were now portrayed as thugs and bullies.

"We used *narcos* tactics against the *narcos*," Eduardo said with a shrug. "It's what they understand. It's all they understand. Now it's me who has to hide."

"Do your new friends suspect? This house. It's a fortress." Levon gestured toward the courtyard wall, the jagged teeth of broken glass glittering.

"It's not so unusual, this level of security. Most of the houses here are like forts. There is no rule of law here now. I'm on my own here and I have children now."

"That's kind of why I'm here, Yayo."

They paused their conversation when the woman from the kitchen stepped out onto the veranda with a tray. She set a pitcher and two tall tumblers filled with ice on the glass-topped table that sat between the two men. She poured sweet tea into each glass and set a wooden bowl of sliced oranges by the pitcher. Levon thanked her, and she mumbled a *de nada* without meeting his gaze. Eduardo offered her a wincing smile and she narrowed her eyes his way before taking the empty tray back inside.

"You were saying, amigo," Eduardo said as he reached for one of the glasses.

Levon related a truncated version of the past year touching on only the most vital details. He had a family himself and they were in danger. He needed help finding the men who were threatening him.

"You suspect these men who came to kill you first came to Mexico and crossed the border?" Eduardo said.

"I can't think of why else they'd steal a car in Laredo."

"They paid coyotes to bring them across." Eduardo held the cold surface of the tumbler to his temple.

"I'd like to talk to the traffickers. I'd like to know how they got paid."

"With the border wide open, the Zetas and Gulf cartel are making more money smuggling people than drugs. There are many *plazas* that do this work."

"And you know them all. You can tell me who I need to see."

"See how? A few friendly questions or the blowtorch and pliers?"

"I'll start with the friendly questions," Levon said, squinting into the sunlight. "I can pay for answers."

"That is dangerous too. Letting these animals know you have money presents its own problems."

"Can you help me, Yayo?"

Eduardo set his drink down on the table untasted. He brushed a fly away from the bowl of orange wedges. He sat back and looked out at the horizon. Far out over the water, a container ship made its way north on the sparkling water.

"I cannot tell you," he said without turning his eyes from the distant boxy shape. "I can only show you."

"That's a lot to ask. I didn't come here looking for that."

"I remember that Good Friday. I remember the men who died. The men we killed."

Levon said nothing.

"That war goes on," Eduardo said.

"Not for you," Levon said.

"No?" Eduardo said and gestured with one hand at the wall that stood between the house and the beach and the crystalline gleam of the glass shards that crowned it.

6

Gunny Leffertz said:
  "When your back's against the wall, climb the wall."

Mirror Lake

SHIVERING in the rear seat of a Chevy Tahoe, Lew Dollinger regretted not dressing warmer. Hard as it was to believe, it actually got colder once he was outside of Anchorage. It was getting dark as the short day came to a close. He'd missed lunch at the Haute Quarter Grill and imagined Kat was pissed.

As he looked out through the salt-glazed window, he was starting to think it never got warm here. It was all black pines and white snow with occasional glimpses of white-capped range tops in the distance. It looked like they might be on Mars.

He had a driver and a guy riding shotgun in the front seats hogging all the heat from the dash vents. He named them Boris and Doris. The driver was a husky Russian with a face like a shovel. The other was a little runt of a guy who seemed effeminate to Lew with his dainty gestures and lilting voice. The smaller guy even held his cigarette like a fag.

The sissy in the passenger seat did most of the talking. It was all aimed at the driver and in Russian. It all sounded like a record being played backward to Lew. He listened anyway, looking for any kind of tone he might pick up. Turned sideways in his seat, Doris never looked back at him. That could be because he had no interest in their passenger or was making an effort not to glance in Lew's direction. Either way, Lew's radar was turned up into the red zone. He didn't like driving to a second locale for his business, but he was from out of town and didn't have a lot of choices.

They'd pulled off something called the Glenn Highway and onto a switchback gravel road. Trees crowded either side of the roadway. The world was reduced to a tunnel of light created by the Tahoe's headlights and the bank of lamps bolted to the cabin roof.

The road ended at a clearing lit by pole lamps. Some steel buildings, a trailer and an honest-to-God log cabin set back at the rear of a snow-covered compound hemmed in all around by dark trees.

Boris and Doris gestured for him to get out of the car and pointed him toward the trailer. They turned to crunch across the ice and gravel for the log cabin. Smoke rose white against the pine tops from a stone chimney. Lew imagined he could smell ham frying and his stomach growled. He'd missed lunch and was probably going to miss dinner too.

He trudged for the trailer. It was raised up on pylons and he gripped the wooden rail as he climbed the slippery steps to a wooden deck set before the door. Lew knocked, and a voice called out from inside. He tried the door, but it was locked or maybe frozen shut. He banged at the door with the flat of his hand. The voice was an irritated rumble now and he could hear footsteps coming closer.

The guy who yanked the door open was more beard than man. Lew was startled by the bushy face that regarded him from the gap in the doorway. It was all nose and teeth, the eyes hidden by horn-rimmed glasses now misted over with condensation.

"Your name is Robert Williams?" Another Russian. "Row-beart Willy-yums."

"Not for long, huh?" Lew said, offering a smile that was not returned.

The interior of the trailer was warmer but not by much. A space heater hummed and crackled in one corner against the chill. The room was paneled and carpeted back in the 1970s. Despite the cold, Lew thought he could smell every minute of its history. Sweat, cigarettes, and garlic. There was a faux leather conversation pit that looked like it belonged in a landfill. An end table was piled with magazines. The only decoration was a borough map of Anchorage tacked to the paneling. He wondered what legit business these reds were using as a front.

Beardo directed him toward a sheet of yellowing poster board duct-taped to the wall. He gestured for Lew to take off his coat and stand against the board.

"What new name you want?" Beardo said as he fiddled with a camera he'd removed from a black canvas case.

"How about Stewart Higgins?" Lew said. He worked with a colored deputy back in the day named Jim-Jack Stewart. And there was a girl back in school named Cissy Higgins he'd been sweet on for a while.

"You write down," Beardo said, nodding toward a clipboard hanging from a hook on the wall. A mini-golf pencil suspended from it on a string.

Beardo took a few shots of Lew as he stood with his head straight and back to the poster board. A couple smiling. A couple not smiling.

"You can wait there," Beardo said, pointing to the L-shaped sofa.

"Hey, you got coffee or like that? Maybe even something stronger," Lew said.

"Later. When I am done." Beardo opened a door at the back of the trailer and Lew caught a glimpse of what looked like an office back there.

It looked warmer in there and Lew almost asked if he could wait inside. But maybe the man didn't like to be watched while he worked.

Lew took a seat at the end of the sofa nearest the space heater and thumbed through some of the magazines. Mostly catalogs for truck parts and some of the vilest porn he'd ever seen with text in languages he didn't recognize.

Cold, bored, hungry, and tired, he looked around the room for further amusements. There was no TV and no radio. He thought of taking a look at the map on the wall. He noticed the clipboard hanging on its hook. He rose from the creaking sofa to step to it.

His new name, Stewart Higgins, was written on the top sheet in block capital letters. He stepped to the office door to listen. One voice speaking inside with pauses now and then to questions.

Lew popped the door's cheeseball lock with one kick from a Larry Mahan boot.

Beardo looked up from behind a desk, a landline phone receiver to his ear. His eyes went wide behind his lenses. Lew scanned the room. An Alaska map. A wooden rack with two shotguns and an umbrella resting on hooks fashioned from the fetlocks of a deer. A New Holland tractor calendar. And, arrayed around the desk, a trio of flat-screen monitors.

On one of the screens was one of Lew's photos taken moments before. It was covered over by a blue grid with a window of text running by it. The text was renewing itself with added text as he watched.

The Russian made to move as Lew threw himself across the desk. Papers, a coffee mug and a printer went flying as both men crashed to the floor in a tangle of wires. Lew took a grip on Beardo's head and slammed it again and again into the carpet. The Russian was clawing at him and calling out what sounded like nasty names. Lew turned his head away to avoid the flailing fingers reaching for a hold on his face.

The floor was too padded to do the damage Lew was looking for. He spared a hand to grab at the fallen coffee mug, a hefty porcelain piece decorated with some two-headed bird kind of symbol. Lew used this to bludgeon Beardo a half dozen times or so. The man collapsed finally, his glasses broken and face smeared with blood from a gash along his hairline. His nose was crushed as well.

Lew picked the phone receiver from the floor and listened to the buzz of a dial tone. He'd heard of the facial recognition programs the feds used. What he saw on the screen damn sure looked like one. He saw his name and personal details in the text window. His real name. His former home address back in Alabama.

He leaped to the gun rack on the wall only to find the shotguns were unloaded. He pulled open desk drawers looking for shells and came up empty. The bottom drawer of a filing cabinet held a Taurus revolver in .44 mag and a box of cartridges.

There was a decorative wooden set of hooks by the door. A key ring with the key to a Chevy hung there. Lew plucked it off on his way to the trailer's main room.

Snatching up his coat, he was out the door and into the cold and dark.

He made his way around so as to keep the trailer between him and the log cabin. Lights glowed in the windows there, but so far, no movement. No one could have heard Beardo's screaming over the stiff wind now tearing through the trees.

Stumbling through drifts, Lew reached a patch of gravel before one of the steel sheds. The main door was unlocked, and he made his way inside. It smelled of oil and rust. He was startled when shop lamps hanging from the ceiling came on to light the interior like a soundstage. He realized they were on motion detectors.

Squatting by a massive snow plow was an old-school Chevy Suburban, two-tone in faded blue and cream. Lew cursed as he saw it. At first, he thought it was up on blocks. Instead of tires, it sat high on triangular shapes that looked like tank treads.

"When in Rome, fuck like a Roman," Lew said under his breath as he climbed the crusted chrome steps up into the cab.

The Chevy came to life with a throbbing roar. There was even the beginning of heated air coming for the dash vents.

Lew dropped from the cab to tab OPEN on a control pad hanging from the ceiling on a cable. The big hangar door shuddered to life as it began sliding upward in a symphony of metal squeals. He was up in the Chevy and gunning it before the door was half open.

He powered out under the door, the whip antennae singing as they struck the door bottom. The bright lights and hellacious noise of that shed door raised the cabin. Lew saw a rectangle of light of an open door and men spilling onto the porch. They pelted over the snow to cut him off, waving arms and shouting mutely, their voices drowned out by the thunder of the Suburban's big eight going all out.

Lew turned hard away from them, looking for the roadway that brought them here. All he could see was trees flashing silver in the swaying arc of his headlights. He could hear the sharp report of gunfire behind him.

No sign of the way he'd come, Lew floored the big machine and aimed for a gap in the trees. The cabin canted, rising and falling as he left the gravel. He fought to maintain a grip on the wheel as his ass left the seat again and again, his head striking the cabin roof.

The sounds of gunfire faded behind him as he fixed his eyes on the way ahead, jinking and slewing between the dark boles of the endless trees that lay before him. Brush slapped at the sides of the cab, and he sideswiped a pine bole or two where the way through became narrow. It was all about distance now not direction. That Tahoe was never going to be able to follow the path of most resistance this tank was traveling over.

Into the long, long night, he made his way through the woods following whatever path took him downward.

Goodbye, Stewart Higgins. It might have been fun.

7

Gunny Leffertz said:

"The shortest distance between two points is the most dangerous place in the world."

Nuevo Laredo

"THE WAY I SEE THIS, you can go at it with a hammer or with a feather," Yayo said as he piloted the Silverado north through the night along a dusty two-lane.

It was a lonely road ambling north between vast fields of grass or soy dotted with houses and barns set well back among trees. At this late hour, there was no traffic. They were well north of Vera Cruz in a desolate part of Mexico, *muy rural.* Four five-gallon gas cans were strapped down against the cab in the truck's bed. It was a long way between Pemex stations out here.

"Which way do you see is best?" Levon said from the passenger seat of the crew cab.

Eduardo shrugged and lifted a hand from the steering wheel to waggle it.

"How does trafficking work along the border?" Levon asked.

"You don't want traffickers. They are a different breed. The most dangerous. We look for a smuggler, a coyote."

"What's the difference?"

"Traffickers smuggle only the unwilling. Women or children who they have bought or stolen. These poor souls do not come to America for a better life. They come to be used."

Levon looked out at the dark fields rushing by. The occasional sprinkle of lights seen through clutches of pin oaks and junipers. He thought of his daughter Hope. She came to Alabama as one of the poor souls Eduardo spoke of.

"THE MEN who came for you would have crossed the border with a first-class outfit," Yayo continued. "They'd pay top dollar. Four adult men traveling together? The risks are high. Usually, men are paired with children, the smaller the better. These get across easily and have a story for the immigration on the Texas side."

"These men would be got-aways. And they'd cross over with their weapons. Unless they were supplied on the US side."

"That would cost them. Money would be paid in advance and the rest once they were across the river. These men, as you say, probably had criminal records in Curaçao. Big risk for the coyote who took them on. What do you hope to learn about this?"

"The outfit that's looking for me is connected through other criminal enterprises," Levon said. "There's only so much anonymity they can count on. This would have been a large transaction. A hundred thousand or more. If the guns I found on them came from this side of the border, you can triple that. And with the level of risk, a degree of trust would be established."

"These killers, they were hires rather than members of the gang who seek you."

"Sure. But I think the money was handled by the boss or bosses. No way they packed those four off with a bag full of cash. Arrangements would have been made ahead of time to pay for the trip and to arm them."

"A prior relationship between the Zetas and the men who are after you."

"This is a big concern with a global reach and deep pockets. The Zetas are all over the world now which means they've probably dealt with this outfit before. Just another component in the underworld network."

"You are hoping that someone here can point you in the right direction. It is a slim hope." Eduardo squinted into the headlight glare stabbing into the dark before them. He turned the wheel to drive around a deer carcass that lay in the right lane. Dark shapes slinked away into the shadows of a ditch that ran alongside the road. Eyes like silver dollars caught the passing light.

"A slim hope is all I've got," Levon said. "Now, tell me about this hammer approach."

THEY REACHED Nuevo Laredo at dawn.

Eighty-five turned into *Avenida Reforma* with border traffic already at a beep and creep pace. Down an off-ramp and soon they were deep in the vast grid of the eastern part of the city. Houses, some with their fronts brightly painted in pastels, lined the streets for block after rectangular block.

There was mostly scattered truck traffic at this hour. School children moved along the walks and gutters, girls in uniform skirts herded in gaggles; each watched over by an older man or woman. Boys running by in starched shirts and ties. All appeared normal but for the pockmarks of bullet holes in many of the shuttered storefronts. The skeletons of burned-out cars sat on sandy lots. From the shade of awnings, slung before the few businesses open at this hour, idle young men sat at tables and watched the Silverado cruise by.

"It is times like this I am glad I wore a mask in the military," Yayo said, eyeing a boy in an oversized T-shirt eyeballing them from his station on a corner.

"It's me they're looking at," Levon said. "Big *gabacho* riding with a homey."

"We make an odd pair. But not so odd as before. With your border open as it is, people from all over the world now come to NL."

"This guy we're meeting? You can trust him?"

"I can rent him," Yayo said with a smirk. "Even you don't carry enough money for trust."

They hooked a right on *Calle Washington*, following across a four-lane avenue past closely-packed houses and empty lots of scrubby pines and baked earth. Eduardo turned the truck into the lot of a Super City supermarket. The steel grates were still pulled down and the interior was dark behind the glass panels that fronted the store. Each window was plastered with bright signs promising *especiales* and *grandes ofertas*.

The Silverado made its way to the rear of the store where two trucks were backed up to an open dock. Men were moving tall stacks of crates and cases into the rear of the store. Eduardo found a spot for the pickup and they exited the AC-cooled cab for the stifling desert heat. The sun was not even over the rooftops and already the windless air had the feel of an oven.

Some young men lounged about a Pepsi machine that hummed in a corner of the dock. They pretended indifference, but it was clear they were studying Levon and Yayo as they climbed the steel steps up to the dock. The boys all wore the uniform of an untucked white-tee that marked them as dangerous as well as serving to hide the pistolas in their waistbands. Whether solicited or hired by force, these kids formed the store's security.

Eduardo parted the plastic strips that hung over the entrance to the store's back area. He held them for Levon to duck under.

The storeroom was cooler than outside. The air was rich with the odors of fruits and vegetables both fresh and spoiled. Past aisles of pallets stacked with colorful produce boxes ten feet high, they found an office tucked in a corner of the hangar-like building. The door was open. Light from inside threw a yellow bar onto the cracked concrete floor.

As they neared the door, a man stepped from the shadows cast by a column of orange crates. He wore a tan uniform shirt, a tie loosely knotted at his open collar. The shirt needed ironing. His face, cheeks pocked with the deep scars of a past skin disorder, needed a shave. A tooled leather equipment belt was worn low on his hips, weighed down by cuffs, pepper spray, radio and a Glock in a flapped holster. His shoulder bore a patch with *Policia Estado de Tamaulipas* embroidered around a coat of arms that included images of livestock, a cross, and an oil rig among other details.

He made a lazy gesture with his fingers and Yayo and Levon stood for a frisk. The cop's search turned up the 1911 that was snug against the small of Levon's back. He plucked it free and waggled it held between thumb and finger before Levon's face.

"*Me gusta esta pistola.*" The cop grinned.

"It's not a gift," Levon answered in Spanish.

The cop gestured with Levon's gun to the open door of the office. Inside, a man sat behind one of two desks piled with inventory manifests and transfer sheets. The man did not stand to greet them. Instead, he sat peeling a banana.

The man behind the desk was in his fifties and wore the same uniform as the frisker. But his shirt was stretched tight over an expansive belly, folds of flesh fell over his collar. His face was bathed in sweat despite the standing fan aimed directly at him. It riffled the edges of the papers heaped upon the desk.

"I am—" Yayo began.

The fat man closed his eyes and waved sausage fingers at them.

"No names," the fat man said, eyes to the meticulous task of removing the strings from the now naked banana. "It's enough that you know men who know me and those same men tell me you are a man of your word."

"Those same men assured me you might be of some help," Yayo said. There would be no names exchanged. No introductions.

"And who is this *gabacho?*" The fat man gestured with the fruit toward Levon.

"You only need to know that he has your money."

"Will he show me this money?"

"Only when he is satisfied."

"And what will satisfy him?" The fat man took a big bite from the end of the banana.

"A few names. A few questions answered. That is all."

"Ask your questions and I will see what I can do."

Yayo told him of the four men who traveled over the border perhaps two weeks previously. The four were island men. Curaçao men. They would have crossed over as a group. They would have wanted discrete entry into the

United States. They would have paid well for this service. Only the most expert *plaza* would do for them.

"Where might I find you to give you these answers to your questions?" the fat man said when Yayo was finished speaking.

"My friend is staying at the Hacienda Grande under the name Templeton," Yayo said.

"Tell him, I will see him tonight then," the fat man said around cheeks packed with banana. "At his hotel."

"*Claro*," Yayo said.

His Colt returned to him; Levon stepped out into the sunlight ahead of Eduardo.

"You know he's planning on fucking you," Yayo said, catching up to Levon as they crossed the lot to the pickup.

"That's why you're going to go back home, Yayo," Levon said.

"You knew this. You meant for this to happen." Yayo tabbed his remote to unlock and start the Silverado.

"We used the feather," Levon said as he slid into the passenger seat. "Now comes the hammer."

"You don't lose me this easy, *gringo*," Yayo said as he cranked the truck to life. "I stay till the ride is over."

8

Gunny Leffertz said:
"See without being seen."

The Hacienda Grande

THE FAT COP and his pock-marked deputy did indeed have names. The fat man was Lieutenant Armando Luis Trabejo of the Tamaulipas State Police. His deputy was a corporal in that same organization who went by Tico "Abollado" Ibanez.

It was well past midnight when they approached the registration desk at the Hacienda. They were in plain clothes now. The lieutenant in an ill-fitting summer weight suit over a black dress shirt. The corporal in a western shirt embroidered with yellow roses against coral across the front and back of the yoke.

Trabejo flashed his badge to the buck-toothed girl manning the counter. He described the *gabacho* they'd met that morning. She pronounced the man's name *tam-pool-tone*. She was able to give them the floor and room number. She did not know if the man was occupying the room currently and he had received no calls.

The two *policia* secured a card that would serve as a master key and went up to the third floor by elevator.

The door to the room opened, they swept inside with handguns drawn. The room was empty. The only sound was the rattle and hum of the air conditioner unit mounted in the wall under the window. A light was on by a bed that appeared to have been slept in.

With an expertise born of years of experience, the two men tossed the room for whatever they could find. It was not much.

The bathroom had been used. There was a gob of errant toothpaste in the sink and a clump of damp towels in the tub. The bathmat was wet. A canvas bag sat atop the dresser. There was nothing of note in it except for a change of clothes. The corporal was disappointed as he had hoped to find the *gabacho's* fine pistola among the room's effects. He dumped the contents of the bag on the floor to sort through them.

The lieutenant snatched the bag from his deputy and removed a clasp knife from his jacket pocket. He slit the seams of the bag and uncovered a wad of American bills, all hundreds, sealed in a plastic bag. He peeled hundred-dollars off the wad. The corporal got four, the lieutenant pocketed the rest.

"He is not here," Tico said, leaning back against the sill of the window. "And we have no idea when he might get back."

"So, we wait," Trabejo said. "And get away from the window, *idiota.*"

FROM A NO-NAME MOTEL off *Calle Simon Bolivar*, Levon watched the pair of state police officers through a motion-activated Go-Pro he'd concealed on the frame of the wall-mounted television. Yayo sat by the window sipping a coffee and smoking. The window was cracked open to allow the smell of the Marlboro to trail out into the night air.

On the screen of a laptop, he could see the men idly awaiting his return. The fat one lay back, propped against pillows and stabbed the remote at the TV. A black revolver lay atop the covers by his hand. The other slouched in a straight-backed chair by the window, fingers parting the blinds to look out on the parking lot. His Glock lay on the sill.

Levon listened as they talked about an upcoming football match between Nuevos Laredo and Guadalajara. The pock-marked one was fidgety. He wondered where the *gabacho* could be. The fat one surmised that the absent guest was with a whore or getting drunk or saying a novena at *Espiritu Santo*. Who knew where he was? Who cared? He would be back for his clothing and his money. For now, enjoy the air conditioning and the pretty *bonitas* on the television.

"Can we have the sound up?" the corporal asked.

"No," the lieutenant said.

"Can we order some food?" The corporal was leafing through the room service booklet.

"*Idiota*," the lieutenant said.

They fell into a sullen silence then and soon both were dozing. The fat one snoring with chins tucked against his chest. The pocked one sprawled in the chair with head back and arms limp at his sides.

Levon realized that he'd learn nothing this way beyond the firm confirmation that this pair meant to ambush him. It could mean they simply meant to hold him up. Were that the case, they would have been happy with the cash they'd found and left already.

Life was not like it was shown in movies and TV shows. As he so often told Merry and Hope. Bad guys did not sit around casually reviewing their plans for anyone who might be eavesdropping. You could listen to hours and hours of inane, idle conversation and never learn anything of value.

That they were staying to brace him in a private place meant something. That they simply didn't pick him up in the course of their normal duties was significant. Propriety never stopped a Mexican cop from putting the bite on anyone. They were looking for more than a quick hit. And they waited until this late hour to come for him.

To Levon that meant they'd looked into the matter of the *gabacho* and the four Curaçao men. They learned that perhaps this was a man of great interest to some very powerful persons. Such a man would be worth something to these persons. Whoever delivered such a valuable prize would be rewarded.

So, this pair of morons decided to freelance by claiming a bounty on Senor Templeton. They were working outside their normal capacity as cops in order to keep the reward to themselves. They grab the *gabacho* in his room and hold him there for a bagman to come collect him.

Levon guessed that these two would wait there until morning. They'd probably taken time off from duty or called in sick. They were out of uniform and off the clock.

He watched them napping in his hotel room. The fat one feebly scratching his balls in his sleep. The other gouging the carpet with the heels of his cowboy boots. Maybe they were dreaming dreams of avarice, of the new world of pleasures and delights that might be theirs when they handed over the *gabacho*.

What a disappointment it would be for them when they woke up in a world of shit.

"Feel like going for a drive?" Levon said, turning to Yayo.

9

Gunny Leffertz said:

"You only need to keep promises to two people. Your mama and yourself."

Vista Hermosa Uno

AT FIRST, he thought it was a heart attack.

Lieutenant Trabejo prayed to the Holy Mother a silent prayer and promised to cut back on the drinking and fatty foods in exchange for a few more years.

When he opened his eyes, he saw that the source of the intense pain in his chest was the knee of the *gabacho* who had visited the Super City earlier. Senor Templeton pressed Trabejo into the mattress with his full weight. The big man was pressing the lieutenant's own Smith and Wesson into his neck.

"Turn over," the *gabacho* said, removing the terrible burden from his chest.

Trabejo did as he was told, rolling over on the bed. The knee pressed into his spine now, hands expertly securing his wrists. He heard the flat rasp of the tie wraps closing. One about his wrists. Another double looped about his thumbs and cinched tight.

He was lifted from the bed to a standing position by the powerful grip of this man Templeton. He saw Tico standing on the side of the bed, hands at his back while the other man, the Mexicano, who'd visited him today applied the plastic cuffs. Tico needed to be supported as he was restrained. He looked dazed and already one side of his face was swelling where his lip had been split. His fancy cowboy shirt was dotted with glistening blood all down the front.

The gabacho went through Trabejo's pockets to retrieve his wallet, car keys, clasp knife, mobile phone and change. These were tossed on the bed to join the contents of his corporal's pockets. All, including their handguns, were scooped up by the *gabacho's* companion and tossed into a plastic bag pulled from the room's waist can.

At the same time, Templeton was tossing his own possessions into the open equipment bag. Trabejo watched in mute fascination as the *gabacho* plucked a tiny device from where it was attached to the side of the wall-mounted TV. It was then that he noticed that both of their unexpected visitors wore blue vinyl gloves. His unease turned to real fright then. Sweat ran down his flanks in a sudden stream.

All of this was accomplished with no words spoken between the two men or their captives. Trabejo spoke now as he and Tico were shoved toward the door.

"Where are we going?" he asked.

"Home," Senor Templeton said in English.

⊏⊐

OUT IN THE rear parking lot of the Hacienda, Levon tabbed the fob remote on the fat one's key chain. A Mercedes sedan, late model, beeped and blinked. A million-peso car on a seven hundred dollar a month salary.

A press of a button popped the trunk as they approached. They had to pull the spare and jack out of the back to make room for the two cops. Yayo helped himself to a Remington pump shotgun he found there. The pair managed to fit inside packed head to toe. The fat one cried out as the lid was brought down. Once shut inside, his shouts were lost in the traffic noise of a nearby overpass.

"Know where this is?" Levon said, holding up the lieutenant's driver's license in the bilious light of the halogens strung along the edges of the lot.

"I can find it," Yayo said, squinting to enter the address on his phone.

"I'll follow you," Levon said, opening the driver's door of the Merc. He'd already brought the engine to life with the remote.

"*Por favor*," Yayo said, grinning. "I've never driven a Benz before."

They exchanged keys and Levon walked to where they'd left the Silverado ten spaces away.

⊏⊐

VISTA HERMOSA WAS a new development south of the city. A tight grid of paved streets lay off 85. Most of the lots were empty. Here and there buildings were under construction. Post-modern *casas* of cinderblock and poured concrete.

The lieutenant's house was among a clutch of four completed houses at the rear of the subdivision. Each was built like a miniature fortress with high courtyard walls and windowless fronts that lined the street. The windows that were visible were fitted with wrought-iron bars.

Driving ahead, Yayo touched a remote clipped to the Mercedes' visor. A motorized door of corrugated steel slid to one side to allow access into the courtyard. The house was dark but for a motion detector lamp that went on when the car pulled up to the garage entrance.

Yayo sat in the air-conditioned quiet and kept eyes on the house. He saw Levon in the side view mirror coming through the gateway on foot. He tabbed the remote on the visor and the gate closed with a rattle and clang. He popped the trunk and joined Levon outside.

"Who lives here with you?" Levon was asking the fat one.

"No one," Trabejo said, his face red and shirt damp with sweat from the hot ride to his house.

"Big house," Levon said.

"His wife left him," the corporal offered.

"Shut up," Trabejo hissed.

"Too many *putas*," the corporal added.

Trabejo jostled in the narrow confines to deliver a kick to the other man's head with a toe of his boot.

"Check it out," Levon said to Yayo who moved to a back door with the key ring rattling in one hand and the pump shotgun in the other.

"You think you will walk away from this?" Trabejo said with a grunt as Levon hauled him upright into a sitting position.

"Who's going to miss you?" Levon said and dragged the man from the trunk.

10

Gunny Leffertz said:

> *"A friend can be anyone for any time. Five minutes or forever. Never turn down help when it's offered. Never turn your back when it's done."*

Malemute Road

THE SUBURBAN WENT DEAD JUST after dawn.

Lew sat pounding the wheel and cursing the Mexicans who'd probably built the car until he saw the fingers of rime ice forming on the windshield. He could see his breath. The heater went when the engine died, and he could feel the cold creeping in under the dash.

He found some worn work gloves in the console. He pulled on two pairs then found he couldn't close his coat and pulled them off again. He found a discarded newspaper on the floor of the truck and stuffed it under the coat as further insulation. He made sure to secure the Taurus under his belt before zipping up. Even bundled as he was, he gasped when the frigid air struck his uncovered face. The coat had a hood, but it was meant more for protection from rain and did little to reduce his loss of body heat.

The Chevy offered no further comforts, so he set out in the same direction he'd been driving in. All night, he'd powered through pine forest and over snow-covered clearings. He followed a downhill course to conserve the quarter tank of gas in the Suburban's tank. Besides, what he knew of backwoods was if you were lost, you looked for water. Follow the water, even the narrowest creek, and you'd come to either a road or houses.

Only this was goddamn Alaska. There was no telling how far he'd have to walk. More damning, how far he could make it dressed for weather at least thirty degrees warmer. That and an empty stomach. Last time he'd had anything to eat was a bear claw and coffee on the cruise ship the morning before. And hadn't even finished the pastry. I'd wrestle a real bear for those last bites right about now, he thought.

And that thought took him to a darker place. There might be a bear, a grizzly, looking at him right now. His hand went to pat the revolver under his coat. His head swiveled back and forth to scan the trees all around. His feet were numb now. He kept his hands pressed under his arms when he didn't need them for balance. His fool, useless cowboy boots were no good on snow. He wound up on his ass every hundred steps or so, the slick leather soles finding no purchase on the frozen surface.

The sky was a lighter gray now as he came to a stream. It was only a crooked white streak running between frost-slick rocks. He could hear water gurgling beneath the ice. That allowed him to determine its direction. He followed a narrow path that ran along above the nearest bank. He squinted toward the woods around him. Despite the heavy overcast, there was a glare off the snow giving him a headache. That and hunger, he supposed.

He came across fresh animal tracks, black against the snow. They looked to be the three-toed prints deer made and always led down to the water's edge. He came across a pyramid of black pellets by the trail that he knew to be bear shit. The height of the pile renewed his vigilance, and he took to walking with one ungloved hand under his coat, fingers tight on the butt of the revolver.

Lew ran over all his decisions made the night before and had to give himself a D minus. Maybe the guy with the Old Testament beard was only checking his identity in order to hold him up for more cash. He could have dealt with that, paid the devil his due. Only he was still troubled by who the Russian might have been on the phone with. In his most pessimistic musings, he imagined it was the nasty little Chinaman on the other end. But he'd only waited on that sofa for twenty minutes or so. Would this guy operating out of a trailer in the middle of fuck-all Alaska have a direct line to someone like the gook? For all Lew knew there could be some kind of jungle telegraph out on him, an underworld APB with a fat purse for whoever handed his lily-white ass over.

Or the guy could have been on the phone with his girl-friend or his mama. Lew damned himself for not listening at the door longer to pick up what language the guy was speaking. Or keeping the guy conscious long enough to ask a few questions.

Now all he could do was wonder if he'd improved his situation by running or only made it worse. If they weren't curious about who he was before they'd damned sure be so now. They'd shake that tree and, sure as shit, that little gook would fall out at some point.

Here he was, on foot, and alone in the country where there were only a few roads cutting through millions and millions of square miles of absolutely nothing but snow and trees. They'd only have to move along those roads looking for a dumbass cracker in cruise wear and shitkickers stepping into the clear.

And that was *if* he made it to any road. Odds were strong he'd die wandering around out here. Just another clueless asshole up from the lower forty-eight to see the sights.

Well, fuck all that, he thought as he walked.

And fuck you. That was for himself for getting his ass into this in the first place.

And fuck you too. That was for God for not stopping him from getting his ass into this in the first place.

As the sun dropped behind the iron mountains and the dark closed in about him, Lew offered a prayer of apology loaded with a lot of fevered promises that he'd keep if only He could see His way clear to magic this Alabama boy to some warm sandy beach somewhere.

———

LUCY HAD NEVER SEEN anything like it. Not in the thirty years since they moved to Knik River from Minnesota.

Riding shotgun while her husband Ed drove, she'd seen grizzlies, caribou, snowshoe rabbits and a moose or two. You needed two sets of eyes on this road, especially at night. You never knew what might charge out into your headlights. Lots of times it was animals big enough to total even their F-150. One time they had to sit idling while a herd of elk moseyed across a two-lane. Whoever rode the suicide seat needed to watch the shoulders for the driver.

But this took the cake, icing and all.

A hitchhiker walking the northbound verge of the Glenn

Highway. *Walking*. A man bent near double against the gale-force wind blowing over the road surface. It was turning loose snow into a swirling mist. A wonder she'd seen the man at all.

"Ed."

"I saw him."

"We have to stop."

"Do we?"

"You know we do."

"Let someone else stop."

"You know there's no one going to come along at this hour."

"You know he's probably drunk. Or high."

"He'll die out there, and you know it."

"You see a car broke down? I didn't see one."

"Could be he skidded off the road."

"Maybe."

"Could be there are others that are hurt."

"Okay."

"You want that on your conscience when you're trying to sleep?"

"I said okay."

"Thank you."

"Only as far as the Three Bears."

"Thank you, Ed."

Ed backed the truck up along the breakdown lane. The man on the road stumbled forward to meet them. Lucy leaned back between the seats to open the rear cab door. The man clambered in and, with some effort, pulled the door shut behind him. He sat quaking on the bench seat, pulling gloves off his hands with his teeth.

"Careful there," Lucy said. "Let those gloves warm up a bit or you'll take the skin off your fingertips."

The man leaned forward, teeth clacking behind cracked lips. He reached his hands out for the console to catch the hot air from the vents. He tried to speak but could not. Lucy was alarmed at his appearance. His face was dead white, like a ghost, with bursts of crimson on the tip of his nose and his cheeks. Another hour out there and he'd have lost that nose.

"Are you alone?" Lucy asked.

The man nodded emphatically.

"We're dropping you off at the Three Bears," Ed said, studying their passenger in the rearview. "You can warm up there and make any calls you need to make."

The man nodded again, trying to form his numb features into a smile.

"No need to thank us," Lucy said.

Lew fought to still his chattering long enough to say "Bless you."

11

Gunny Leffertz said:

"It's a matter of when but everybody talks."

Vista Hermosa Dos

LIEUTENANT ARMANDO LUIS TRABEJO shivered in the bathtub in the darkness of his own spacious master bath. He was naked but for his cowboy boots as they'd cut his clothes from him using a retractable knife. His ankles were now bound tightly together with tie wraps. His fine jacket and pants lay in a tattered heap on the tiles. The porcelain floor of the tub was ice cold on his bare back and rump. A frigid draft dropped on him from the ceiling vents. The *gabacho* and his Mexicano companion had cranked the AC to max.

Trabejo knew that his electric bill was the least of his

worries right now. They had separated him from Tico immediately upon entering the house. He knew this tactic. After many years of being a policeman, he knew it well. If you wanted the truth, you needed to compare stories. They might talk to Tico then talk to him. They would know who was lying and who was not. Who told the truth first would be rewarded.

He hoped they would talk to him first. He sat trembling in the tub under the icy draft. Listening hard, he heard only silence from the depths of the house. There was no way to tell if this was a good thing or a bad thing. He weighed his options as he waited. He considered his choices, what approach to take with these men. Bravado or compromise.

Eventually, he landed on compromise. Make a deal. The ease at which these men had taken him and Tico, the economy of effort and assured movements told him these were professionals. These were not men to be bluffed or easily fooled.

The only question, the most troubling of all, was what side of the law did these men fall upon? Not that it made a great deal of difference here in Mexico. But the difference might be just enough to keep him alive.

He surmised that they were soldiers or law enforcement. They showed no badges. They did not speak to others via radio. When *Norte Americanos* came, they came in numbers not in pairs. It could be that this pair were freelancers looking to extort or steal from the *plazas*. This was his most fervent wish. Such men would be open to a deal, a partnership even.

Only, as he sadly had to admit to himself, it was far more probable that they were bandidos. Bold ones, to be sure. Who would prey on police as their first choice?

That brought him to a most unpleasant conclusion. These men were working for someone. They were agents of a *plaza* or a cartel. Perhaps, without meaning to, Trabejo had become a pawn in a war between powerful forces. Sure, he was on the payroll of the Zetas and they held the whole state in their grip. But the history of Mexico over the past four decades was the shift in power between the state and the *narcos*. Long ago, the cartels won this war and now had only each other for competition. Things had been quiet for many years, but tensions were always there beneath the surface like tectonic plates, building and building pressures until the earth erupted.

Towns, whole states, changed hands when the fight for control of the warehouses, tunnels, trucks, and routes along the border turned bloody. Even someone like an officer of the *policia estatal* could find himself crushed between such titanic forces.

Trabejo was startled out of his reverie by a sudden sound from deeper in the house. It was a single thunderous roar. Footsteps approached, and he winced as the lights came on. The *gabacho* stepped to the side of the tub. The Mexicano took a seat on the toilet lid, the shotgun held across his knees. The oily sulfur smell of the recently fired weapon filled the room.

"Your *subalterno* thought he could bullshit us," the big man said, a yellow work boot resting on the lip of the tub. "I hope you're smarter than that."

The lieutenant nodded mutely, his face darkening as a stream of piss ran from his crotch to the drain.

———

TRABEJO WAS SMARTER and more talkative than his corporal.

The lieutenant had made some calls and texted around after speaking to them that morning in the office behind the supermarket. He shared all he had learned with the big man.

Four men, as described to him by the *gabacho's* Mexican, had crossed over into Texas ten days earlier.

They were serious men. Dark men. Experienced like soldiers. Well-armed and equipped, the lieutenant's informants told him. A large fee had been paid to get these men over the border. Only the best outfit could handle such a task. A gang of coyotes with a *jefe* who called himself Serpiente. The Snake. This was not the usual *plaza* made up of opportunists and small-time hustlers.

Serpiente was connected, a first or second cousin to one of the core council members of the Zetas. Keeping it in the family. When a package, drugs, guns, persons, had to get into the United States absolutely free of interference, Snake's outfit was the most trusted.

"You know there will be police looking for me when I do not report for work in the morning," Trabejo said, fighting to keep the quaver from his voice. Telling himself the tremble came from the cold and not his fear.

"We called your department," the big man said. "You told them you and your amigo were taking a few days off."

Trabejo sighed.

"How was the crossing to be made?" the big man asked.

"I don't know. It would not be a river crossing. Serpiente has tunnels. He charges others tolls to use them. Perhaps one of them."

"Do you know where the tunnels are?"

"That's not something they would share with me. It would cause suspicion if I asked about them."

"Didn't they wonder why you were asking about the four islanders?"

"I asked as a police matter. I told my *informante* that the *federales* were around asking questions. If it got back to Serpiente he would think I was only looking for a bite in exchange for protecting him."

"By misdirecting the *federales*."

"*Si.*" Trabejo dipped his head in a sullen nod.

"You've done business with this *plaza* in the past."

"*Si.*"

"There's a level of trust?"

"As much trust as they can have in the police. Or one outside the family."

The big man left the room without a word. His Mexicano went with him. They closed the door behind them.

Trabejo shivered in the tub. The puddle of urine he sat in was cold on his ass and shriveled balls. His hands, pinned behind his back, were numb and throbbing.

The Mexicano returned alone. He had a loose bundle of clothes under his arm that he tossed on top of the toilet tank. The Mexican snapped open a clasp knife, it was Trabejo's own. He used it to cut the bands around Trabejo's ankles. He shoved Trabejo forward to free his thumbs and wrists.

"Clean yourself up and get dressed," the Mexican said and left him alone to do so.

Trabejo did as he was told, struggling to clamber from the tub on legs like rubber. His hands ached as the circulation returned to them. He washed himself, dried off and sat on the toilet seat to pull his boots off so he could dress in the shirt and pants the Mexican had brought him. A white dress shirt and cargo shorts. They were his own clothing taken from a closet in the bedroom in which he slept.

Once he had his boots back on, he rapped on the door to let his captors know he was ready. The Mexicano opened the door and gestured for him to exit the room. He directed Trabejo toward the rear of the house with a shove.

The big man was leaning against a counter in the kitchen, a mug of freshly made coffee in his hand. The shotgun lay on the counter behind him.

The Mexican shoved Trabejo into a chair at the kitchen table across from his corporal. Tico sat on the other side of the table from him with a mug of coffee of his own, looking like a child in one of Trabejo's camp shirts several sizes too big for him.

"You thought they'd killed me?" Tico said with a stupid grin on his face.

"I *prayed* they'd killed you," Trabejo groused.

Gunny Leffertz said:

"One minute you're praying to Jesus to save your ass. The next you're bitching there's not enough ice in your Coke."

Outside Chugiak

THE THREE BEARS turned out to be the biggest truck stop Lew Dollinger had ever seen.

It had pump islands on three sides and, at the center, a store half the size of a Wal-Mart. Part of that was a diner and Lew took a seat in a booth nearest a big porcelain wood stove. The waitress found him there, hunched over a placemat menu.

"Coffee to start?" she said, trying not to stare in wonder at the near-frozen customer in booth eight. He had to be the whitest white man she'd ever seen in her life. And his clothes, or lack of, made him out to be a tourist or an escaped mental patient.

She was a pretty enough girl, prettier if she'd seen an orthodontist. But she had a nice, if crooked, smile and a spray of freckles over her nose and cheeks.

"Bring a potload," Lew said, struggling to keep the quaver from his voice. "And you got anything to fortify it?"

"I think I can come up with something," she said and made her way back to the kitchen.

Lew looked the place over while he cautiously peeled off the work gloves. The nice folks who dropped him off warned him again about not being in too much of a hurry to get the gloves off. Well, the wife was nice anyway. Lew had a strong suspicion the husband was operating against his better judgment. Lew held no grudge. Hell, *he* wouldn't have picked *him* up either.

The truck stop was a brightly lit cavern with a high steel roof decorated all around with antlers of all kinds. It had aisles of the usual truck stop stuff. Junk food, sodas, beer and groceries. There was a row of pinball and arcade games. A Redbox DVD dispenser. Racks of clothing. And an aisle of electronics gear. A magazine stand. And a row of what had to be the last payphones in existence. The parts department looked like you could build yourself a whole new truck from what they had piled on shelf units that nearly reached the ceiling.

He had the last glove off by the time the waitress returned with a coffee mug and an insulated carafe.

"There's a stiff shot of Old Bostonian in there," she said with a wink. "Only don't go tellin' no one, or they'll all want the same."

"I can keep a secret like no one else," Lew said and managed a smile.

She poured him a mug full, and he wrapped the sore

fingers of both hands around it to feel the heat radiating out through the ceramic.

"You thought of what else you might like?" she said.

"You serving breakfast?"

"Twenty-four hours a day," she said with some pride.

Lew ordered four eggs over easy, a double serving of sausage, another of bacon, biscuits and gravy, and a pile of buttered toast. He forced himself not to wolf it all down. Hungry as he was, starved even, he'd likely throw it all up. He took small bites and washed it down with sweet coffee that seemed to restore him more and more with each sip.

"Taking your time, I see," the waitress said, returning to take away empty plates.

"Got nowhere special to be."

"It's okay. This hour most of the tables are empty anyway."

She was right. There were a few lone wolves like him at a couple of booths and a quartet of what he assumed were long-haul drivers around a table.

"This place have showers?" he asked.

"Free to customers in the back." She raised a hand to the rear of the building. "I suggest you buy your own bar of soap though. Manager buys some wicked shit by the gallon. You don't want that."

"Thanks for the advice," Lew said as he gnawed at a toast wedge.

"And you might want to pick yourself up some warmer clothes. Where'd you think you were anyway?"

"I might have got on the wrong cruise." He grinned.

"You sure got off at the wrong place." She grinned back.

"The showers. They hot?"

"Steaming."

"Always warmer with two."

"I'll get your check." She blushed, the freckles turning crimson, but her smile was still in place.

He finished up his breakfast and paid in cash leaving the waitress a twenty. On his way back to the showers, he picked up a pack of underwear and another of t-shirts. A couple of heavy flannel-lined shirts and a new pair of jeans. His khakis were ripped by brush. In addition, he bought a pair of Timberlands and some wool socks to go with them as well as a thick down coat with an insulated hood. The guy at the counter suggested gloves and would he want a bag to carry all this stuff in?

It all came to near seven hundred bucks at truck stop prices, but Lew paid it gladly. He peeled off hundreds from his ready roll. The counter man threw in a used canvas carry-all for free. Lew left all but the change of clothes he'd need with the counter man and walked back to the showers.

The showers were in private rooms with locking doors. Lew stripped out of his clothes and stuffed them all, even the Larry Mahans, into a trash bin. His braided leather Noconas belt he kept. He set the Taurus and box of shells on the sink counter and hung his money belt on a hook.

He helped himself to a twenty-minute shower, luxuriating under the needle spray as the last of the aches in his hands, legs, and feet melted away. The room was fogged with steam as he emerged from the shower booth. He could still feel a tingle in his fingers and toes as he toweled off. That sensation might take a while to subside, he supposed. Damned lucky he still had all his digits after walking across half the Yukon.

After tearing the tags off the clothes, he slipped them on and felt renewed. Once dressed, he looked in the mirror and thought he resembled a hairless Dollar Store Paul Bunyan. He untucked the black and red plaid flannel shirt so as to conceal the revolver against his back. The box of cartridges he stuffed into the plastic shopping bag with the leftover pairs of underwear and socks.

In no particular hurry, he idled on his way back to the

sales counter, browsing the magazine aisle but finding only gun magazines and some Sudoku puzzle books. What happened to truck drivers? He could recall when a place like this would always have a row of titty magazines. Lew thumbed through a magazine that specialized in handguns and skimmed a review of the Taurus that lay nestled hard against his spine. The reviewer thought it to be a poor imitation of a Smith and Wesson and informed Lew that it was a product of Brazil. Lew thought the reviewer was being picayune, a wheelgun being a wheelgun and who cared where it came from so long as the bullets came out the right end.

He replaced the magazine at the front of the stack to make his way to the sales counter and pick up his goods, considering adding a wool cap to his purchases. Lew stopped by a display of toques to glance at one of the entrances across the broad front of the building. Two men were stepping inside walking side by side. Their eyes moving and heads turning to take in the whole place.

Boris and Doris.

13

Los Garza

CRISTOBEL BRAVO TOOK great pride in his humility.

At thirty-two, he was a successful businessman with famous friends and fifteen children, six of whom bore his last name. He still had his hair, his belly was still flat, and he was tall for an Indio at five foot nine. His custom Tacovas boots brought him to six.

And yet, for all the gifts that God had blessed him with and those he took for himself, he never forgot where he came from.

Born dirt poor in the most desperate part of Guadalajara, a place famous for its desperation, Cristo worked his way up from runner to mule to coyote. In the days of more stringent supervision of the border, he was caught driving a van packed with Guats at the San Luis crossing. That led to five years spent at La Mesa, where his real education began. Released at age twenty-four, he took the lessons learned inside the prison and applied them to what he called his second life.

Now he was the alpha coyote with a pack of hundreds working for him on both sides of the Rio Grande. His tunnels allowed his crews to move freely back and forth between Laredo and Nuevo Laredo. Even more profitable were the tolls he charged others for their use.

In truth, his real troubles were never with the law or rival *plazas*. These he dealt with by threats and bribes and the occasional use of a pig farm in the hills above El Cenzio. His greatest concern was always the physical storage of all the cash he amassed each day. It had to be bundled and secreted in vaults and safes all around the city. Even after paying up a portion to his cousins in the Zetas, the sheer bulk of it was daunting.

Keeping track of his wealth was the work of his most trusted associates, his older brother Gustavo and two first cousins Vico and Robi. The three of them did nothing but complain about this work. The counting. The bundling. The ongoing search for more secure storage for the bags, boxes and palettes of Yankee dollars that came his way each week. He would scold them for their bitching. He would remind them that, once upon a time, a pocketful of pesos would have been a dream come true for them. Now they handled millions and were well paid to do so.

For all of this, his good fortune, his good luck and his good looks, Cristo was proud that he had never succumbed to the temptations of arrogance or vanity. Except for the indulgence of his ostrich skin Tacovas, he dressed like any working man. He wore no gold or jewels. No rings or bracelets or chains as was common among his class of narco. Only a simple silver crucifix given to him by his mother that hung from a strip of braided leather about his neck. A carefully faded work shirt and jeans were his usual costume. Not even a fancy mother-of-pearl or gold belt buckle. Too prideful. Too ostentatious.

He even drove a Toyota pickup that was five years old,

the paint on its hood peeling from heat of the desert sun. Drove it himself, in fact. Though he was always accompanied by one or more bodyguards. There was a point at which modesty became impractical, even foolish.

His home was a humble rancho in the Los Aztecas section though he owned many more houses and condos about the city where several of his ex-wives and girlfriends lived with his children. There were many places he could call home, many places where he was welcome.

If he allowed himself any pride at all it was for the businesses he'd built all across the state. These were legitimate, at least on paper, concerns purchased with cash gathered from smuggling and leases. And, though they were only meant to provide yet another means of stowing his cash, many of them turned a profit. And these funds could be legitimately deposited in a bank.

He owned, through blind trusts, holding companies and trusted cousins, aunts, uncles, a nephew, and two of his sisters, ran garages, appliance stores, apartment buildings, bars, laundromats, two car dealerships, and portion of a cable television company.

But, as unpretentious as he was and as fulfilled by his own humbleness as he was, he was still stirred to real pride by his most favorite of the businesses he owned. They were a chain of three bakery and coffee shops he'd named *Panadería de Angel*. He'd named them himself after the woman in the Starbucks logo. He had no idea what a Starbuck was and mistook the mermaid in the logo for an angel.

The three stores, dotted about Nuevos Laredo, served as an oasis for him. They were managed by his little sister Lupita, and she had done an excellent job, under his close direction, of recreating the hipster vibe of a real *Norte Americano* coffee shop even down to the drive-through window and cool jazz on the sound system.

More and more, his regular stops at one of the *panaderias*

was the highlight of his mornings. Though he was careful never to visit the same one two days in a row or even on the same day of the week as a previous visit. Patterns were an unwelcome risk in the life of an original gangster, as he'd been schooled by the *viejos* back at *La Mesa*. This was why he never laid his head down in the same place two nights in succession. He was the *primo grande* of a thriving plaza. Such a man, even a man who lived as plainly as he, was a constant target.

Cristobal turned the Toyota off *Calle Zapata* and onto the lot of the *panaderia*. He was pleased to see a boy hosing the dust from the walkway. Another pulled and tied bags of trash from the receptacles set before the entrance.

Zorro, so named because he was far from handsome, accompanied him into the store. His other bodyguard, Guapo, so named because he was even more unsightly, remained with the truck. This pair were loyal childhood friends of Cristo's and well paid to remain so.

It was midmorning and most of the booths and tables were empty. A pair of old men played chess at a back booth. A serious young man sat bent over an open laptop. A pair of girls chatted and laughed, their eyes fixed on the phones in their hands rather than on one another. This brought a smile to Cristo's face. More than a place to eat sweets and swill coffee, his *panaderia* had become part of the community.

A teenage boy was at the counter and took his and Zorro's order. A plain black coffee for Cristo, an espresso, and a gooey yoyo for his man. The boy took the fruit-filled pastry from the display case with his bare hand to put it on a plate.

"You are fired," Cristo said through clenched teeth.

The boy looked at him, uncomprehending.

"I said, get out of here. Now." Cristo jerked his head toward the door.

The boy backed away, terror in his eyes.

"*Pronto*," Cristo rumbled.

His eyes locked on Cristobal as one might watch a coiled snake, the boy edged along the counter and toward the opening into the main room.

Cristo crossed the tiles in three strides to meet him at the door.

"Your apron, *pendejo*." Cristo yanked at the front of the boy's apron. The boy hurriedly undid the knot at his back even as the angry visitor was tugging it off him. A kick from the toe of a Tacova propelled the kid stumbling into the lot. Leaning on the pickup, Guapo let out a donkey bray of laughter at the sight.

The girls in the booth held their phones out to capture the moment.

Lupita came from the office at the sound of her brother's voice.

"What the fuck, Cristo?" she shouted as she rounded the display case.

"He served Zorro a pastry with his filthy hands," Cristo replied coolly, his elan returning after his sudden flash of temper. "And his apron was soiled and why would you put someone with acne that bad where customers could see him?"

"This is my place to run," she seethed, stabbing his chest with a beautifully manicured nail. "You promised I would do this my way."

"Only so long as you didn't fuck it up."

"Now I have to work the counter! Stephan was here till four and I have errands to run!"

"Bring in one of those boys on the lot then. They look like they know how to work."

"Those peons? I pay them in day-old *orejas* to clean the lot. They don't even have proper shoes!"

"I only came in for coffee," Cristo said, working up a smile for his little sister.

He touched her shoulder and lowered his eyes in submission. She brushed away his hand though she returned the smile.

"It is a good thing you came," she said, taking the apron from his hand and tying it about her waist.

"Yes?"

"A man came here asking for you. He said a man named Trabejo, a police, sent him."

"What kind of man?" Cristo's eyes narrowed as he watched his sister draw his and Zorro's drinks.

"A Ukrainian."

"How do you know he was Ukrainian?"

"He told me so."

"What was his name, *hermana?*"

"I don't know. A Ukrainian name."

"What did he want with me?"

"He left you something," she said as she presented them with their cups and a fresh yoyo upon a sheet of waxed paper.

"Lupe..." he sighed, his patience wearing thin.

"Here," she said, popping open the cash register and retrieving a tiny wad of paper from a change drawer.

He unfolded the paper to find what looked like a dull white stone at the center. It was an unpolished rock smaller than the tip of his little finger. He tapped it on the glass atop the display cabinet.

"Is it drugs?" Lupita said, her voice hushed. "Because you promised me..."

"It's not drugs," he said, annoyed, as he dragged an edge on the stone over the glass leaving a long white line scored in the surface.

Lupita goggled at the fresh scar in the glass.

"Where did this man say I could find him?" Serpiente said, dropping the stone into the breast pocket of his humble workingman's shirt.

14

Gunny Leffertz said:

> *"Sometimes all you can do is hope tomorrow turns out better."*

The surveillance video at the Three Bears Shell told most of the story.

The incident, according to the timestamp, started at 2:41 a.m.

Two Caucasian males enter through the bank of doors that front the store. They separate to walk the aisles. Their demeanor suggests that they are not browsing for anything in particular. Both men seem to be looking over the tops of the displays rather than at the goods on the shelves and pegs.

A third man in a bright red shirt, also Caucasian, can be seen ducked low to move between aisles.

The shooting starts at 2:43 with the shorter of the two

men opening fire. His fire is not random. He appears to be clearly aiming in the direction of the man in the red shirt. His partner moves quickly to the front of the store where he intercepts red shirt attempting to exit onto the parking lot. An exchange of gunfire ends with the taller of the visitors collapsing into a Little Debbie display and onto the floor where he remains for the rest of the video's run.

The cameras out on the pump islands pick up the rest.

Red shirt runs between cars pulled up to the entrance to make a straight line toward the pump islands directly opposite the front entrance. He slips and falls, going sprawling on the lot. At this time the shorter of the two visitors exits the store in pursuit. There is another exchange of gunfire with the man in the red shirt firing from a supine position where he has fallen and the shorter of the two visitors firing as he runs.

The shorter man is flung from his feet and appears to lose his grip on his weapon. Red shirt rises then to walk to where the shorter man is trying to rise to his knees without success. Red shirt appears to be reloading his handgun, a revolver, after which he fires two more rounds into the fallen man who collapses to the ground where he lies unmoving.

Red Shirt then runs across the lot into a blind spot but re-emerges into camera view on the north face of the store where he runs between the semis gassing up at the diesel islands. The last image of him has red shirt moving past dumpsters and out of the range of the cameras.

At 3:12 a.m., the suspect, now identified as Robert Williams of Lacoste, Louisiana, was apprehended by state troopers. He was found hiding under the Birchwood Loop Road overpass.

"YOU KNOW those two men you shot?" Detective Sergeant Wayne Dryer, Anchorage Police Department asked.

"Never saw them a day in my life," the man across the table answered. He was sipping coffee from a paper cup with some difficulty as both his wrists were cuffed and the chain run through a steel U-bolt welded to the tabletop. The guy's near albino coloring was accented by the blossom of broken blood vessels across his nose and chin.

"They seemed to know you."

"Well, they were mistaken then, I suppose."

"You had no prior association with either of them."

"No, sir."

"No cause to kill either of them. Because that's what you did."

"I thought they might be robbing the place. I was doing what any citizen should do."

"Does that include the two rounds to the head for the last man?"

"I felt he still posed a threat to myself and others, sir."

That last was about the biggest load of horseshit DS Dryer had ever heard. Everything about this guy was horseshit. And his language, his choice of words, suggested he'd been in trouble before. For now, his ID was holding up. For now. But everything about this guy was wrong from his honey-pie accent to his squirrelly eyes and his newly-bought clothes.

"I'm stepping out a minute," Dryer said, pushing away from the interrogation table.

"I'll be right here," Lew said, offering as much of a toast with his cup as he could given his restraints.

Dryer left the interrogation room for the squad bullpen.

"What do we have on the deceased?" he said to a pair of men seated on either side of the partner's desk they shared.

"ID says they're Carl Steven Welles and Mark Thomas Paulson out of Portland," Detective Ira Waska said, reading from his terminal. "Driver's licenses and social security. Both SS cards look new to me. Bogus. We're waiting on prints."

"Their guns turn up as legal purchases in Michigan," Officer Dean Treat said from memory. "Both registered to a Howard Louis Neff of Dearborn."

"You call him?" Dryer asked.

"I talked to his wife," Dean said. "He passed away two years ago. She didn't know anything about the guns. Told me he never owned one."

"And the revolver?"

"That apparently was in Mr. Neff's secret firearms collection too."

"So, this Williams did know the two he killed. They came looking for him and he took them down. How's *his* ID holding up?"

Ira shrugged. "We're running his prints too. Carol said she'd get them to us as soon as we hear back."

"He could claim self-defense. Stand your ground," Dean said, nodding toward his own monitor that displayed a live image of Lew hunched over the steel table sipping coffee.

"Horseshit," Dryer said. "That was a shoot-out."

"They fired first."

"I'd agree with you right up till he puts the double tap in the little one's head. That was murder."

"Jury might take his side. Especially if the two dead guys come up dirty."

"Peas in a pod," Dryer said and turned back toward the interrogation room.

—

"YOU THOUGHT about changing your story, Mr. Williams?"

"I was gonna ask about lunch."

"The gun you used. Did you know it was registered to the same owner as those two strangers you killed?"

"Well, color me surprised."

"This doesn't look like a random event. This looks to me like score settling. These two came looking for you and you wound up on top."

"Still makes it self-defense."

"That's not the whole story."

Dryer's cell pinged and he plucked it off his belt to thumb it to life. He studied the screen, scrolling through text and photos. He held the phone out for Lew to squint at. There were the faces, mug shots, of two men there.

"Mikhail Gustav Zhelenkov and Boris Ivan Petrov. Past charges in Detroit and Indianapolis for statutory rape, armed assault, possession, and trafficking among other charges. I'm betting your prints will tell a tale as well." Dryer scrolled on.

Hot damn, one of them *was* named Boris, Lew thought as Dryer studied the screen. Dryer's eyebrows shot up and he set the phone down to study Lew.

"You were a law officer in Alabama. Sheriff's deputy for eight years."

"I found more gainful employment in the private sector."

"Doing what?"

"This and that. Private security. Some investigating,"

"I don't see a private investigator license."

"It was mostly favors for friends."

"Were those Russians your friends?"

"Not anymore. Can we discuss lunch now?"

"After you're charged. Do I need to read your rights, Mr. Dollinger?" Dryer put special emphasis on the last.

"I can read them to myself. Give me something to do in my cell during the long evenings."

"This a second-degree murder at the worst and you know it. That's a long time inside for you."

"Now that we got that out of the way, can I have a phone call?"

"Do you have a lawyer?"

"There ain't a lawyer on God's green earth can get me out of this," Lew smiled, eyes lowered.

"You gonna call the Kremlin then?" Dryer said, amused.

"I was thinking more like a federal agency." Lew looked up, the smile still fixed in place but his eyes hard. "And maybe something from that candy machine I saw on the way in here."

15

Gunny Leffertz said:

"The trick to lying is you got to believe the lie yourself."

Palacios

LEVON INSISTED they meet in a public place.

He chose a galleria on *Calle Zaragoza*. It was a run-down collection of shops and kiosks under a sheet metal roof. They sold knockoff goods, cheap jewelry, and phones. The meet was to happen in a food court that was arranged like the ones in every mall in the USA. Except it was filthy and all of the fast-food chain names were a little off. Pizza House. Sub Street. Burger Royal.

He paid for a bottled tea at one of the stalls and took a seat at a table where he could watch both entry doors. Ceiling fans mounted in the rafters above stirred the steamy air. Most of the tables were occupied though few people were eating. The crowd was a mix from all over the world, a babel of languages creating an ambient sound. He heard snippets of Bantu, Urdu, and Hindi. Each group sat in cliques to themselves. Some on the steps that led to an upper level. Those that didn't have a canvas bag or rolling case clutched a plastic shopping bag in their hands.

This was a part of the latest caravan that had come to the border up through the Darien Gap. The galleria was a waiting room for them while they killed time until their time to cross. Probably some had not yet negotiated the final leg over the river. A few would have been abandoned here by their coyotes after foolishly paying the full fare in advance.

A silhouette loomed out of the sun's glare coming through the street exit. The man stopped inside the doors to allow his eyes to adjust to the interior gloom. This guy wasn't one of the usual crowd that visited here.

He wore a red silk shirt untucked and only partly buttoned. The open collar showed off the circlets of a couple of gold chains. Rings caught the light of flickering fluorescents as he lifted a hand to remove a pair of black-lensed Oakleys from his broad nose. The guy squinted around the tables and Levon stood to show where he was seated.

The guy joined him. An unattractive guy with jowls visible through a halfhearted attempt at a goatee. Even untucked, the shirt was stretched taut over a generous belly.

"You are the Ukrainian?" the guy said.

"You're not the Snake," Levon replied in his flat, unaccented Spanish.

"He does not like to meet in such places." The guy looked around, gold-capped teeth showing through lips parted in a smirk.

"So, how are we to do business?"

The guy in red leaned forward to retrieve something from his back pocket. Under the tabletop, Levon tapped a finger on the trigger guard of the 1911 held atop his knee. The guy held up a phone for him to see before tabbing a number. He held the screen up to Levon once more and a face appeared. It was a dark man with even features.

"You have diamonds," the man on the phone said.

"You're the man I contacted," Levon said. "You're the man I was sent to see."

"The quality of the stone you left me is good. The others are like this one?"

"I guarantee they are three to four carats uncut weight. All in the VVS2 to VS1 range."

"Natural stones then. I was expecting industrial diamonds from a Russian."

"I am not Russian," Levon said.

"*Lo siento*," the man on the phone said. "You are Ukrainian."

"Yes," Levon lied.

"What do you want in exchange for these?"

"I need guaranteed passage into the United States. I have been told you can provide this."

"How far are you traveling? Do you have a destination?"

"Does that matter to you?"

"Only in that I could recommend the services of ones I know if you require further transportation."

"I only need to get over the border. I can make my own arrangements from there."

"Then, let me see," the man on the phone moved his face out of range of the camera for a moment then returned. "I can do this for ten stones like the one you left me."

"Five."

"Seven and this is as low as I go."

"Only if we meet. I was told to deal with you directly. I was told you are a man of your word."

"I would not survive long in this business were I not. Zorro will bring you to me. You will ride with him."

The call ended. The screen turned to a menu with a background of a naked woman lying with arched back upon a tiger skin.

"Are you ready?" Zorro said.

Levon replaced the automatic against the small of his back as he rose. The other man weaved between tables, leading Levon back the way he'd come.

The shade of the portico that ran down one wall of the galleria was filled with clumps of people seated or lying on the sidewalk. Some dozed while others shooed flies from them with folded newspapers. Those who were awake watched the passing traffic with dull eyes, indifferent to their surroundings. Along the curb, young boys hawked sodas and bottled water from tubs filled with melted ice now turned to lukewarm soup in the afternoon heat. They sold to the cars stopped at the red light. They made no effort to move wares to those sweating in the shade. These *extranjeros* were either penniless or miserly with what funds they had.

Levon followed the man in red silk across an intersection crowded with truck, car, and scooter traffic to an unpaved parking lot on the opposite corner. In the second row was a plain white van with a faded logo for a tire company along its side panels.

"You ride in the back," the man in red said, keys jangling in his beringed fingers. "Gringos draw attention."

Levon hesitated. A moment of doubt. The sense that he was stepping through a threshold. He tamped it down. This was the way forward. The way he'd chosen. It was something he had to do; something there was no walking away from.

The man in red unlocked the rear doors and swung one of them open.

Two men sat on the floor of the van against one wall. Lieutenant Trabejo and Corporal Ibanez. Their hands were drawn behind them. Their faces bore the expressions of men who knew they were lost. On the floor of the van lay another figure, bound hands and feet. This man lay still. Bare to the waist and shoeless. The sole of one of his feet crusted black with dried blood.

Yayo Lugo.

Levon's hand snaked under his shirt for the checkered grip of his 1911. His arm was pressed hard against his back. The weight of two men shoved him against the closed door of the van with brutal force. A knee slammed into the small of his back. His face was pressed against the searing hot steel. He could not free his arm. A kick forced his legs apart and he was driven to his knees. His wrist was pressed up toward his shoulders until he felt a pop. His arm went numb, and he was belly down on the gravel with two men atop him.

A shadow fell over him then and he twisted his head to see the shape of a man crouched by him, a silhouetted form blacking the sun.

"You wanted to meet me," said the voice of the man on the phone. "Not so much as I wanted to meet you."

16

Las Colinas Sobre El Cenzio

SY HANCOCK, two hollers over from the house he grew up in, raised pigs. When the wind was right, the stink of the place came over the pine tops. Especially on the hotter days. So, Levon knew the unique odors of a pig farm. The cloying stench of shit and piss filled the back of the van long before the hour drive over partly paved roads came to a stop.

Yayo was unconscious for the length of the ride. He did not respond to Levon's questions. He'd been beaten severely enough to cause him to bleed from the ears. Levon thought he might be comatose; might never wake up. His feet showed signs of what they'd put him through. The skin of the sole of his right foot had been sliced away. Strips of exposed tendons and bone were visible through a dark film of dried blood.

Not that Yayo could have added to what Levon already knew to be true. It was a mistake to drop the corrupt rurales lieutenant's name. Part of Serpiente's background check on this Ukrainian stranger would be a visit to Trabejo. Yayo was caught by surprise, overwhelmed.

The van doors were jerked open, and the pair of cops were dragged out first. Levon was gripped by the tie wraps that bound his ankles and pulled along the floor of the van into the open air. Yayo was rolled out to drop as lifeless as a rice sack to the packed earth of a muddy farmyard. It was getting on to evening, the sky darkening over the surrounding hills.

A trio of steel buildings were set around the yard with one end of the open area dominated by a long structure with open sides under a steel roof. This was enclosed by wooden fencing. The hog pens covered an acre of ground. The sour funk from the pens filled the air. The grunts of porkers could be heard over the fence.

One of the men crouched to cut Levon's ankles free. Two more men pulled him to stand on his feet. A pimped-out Lincoln SUV on knobby tires pulled into the yard from between two buildings. Cristobel Bravo stepped from the glare of the row of lamps set atop the SUV's cab.

"Free their hands as well," Cristo said. The two men from the van did as they were told while other men, Levon counted four more that he could see, stood watching, shotguns in their hands. The shotgun men wore high rubber boots and farmer overalls.

"Now, you will strip," Cristo said when Levon and the two cops had been cut free. Yayo's ties had also been cut away.

Trabejo opened his mouth to plead his case, a smile fixed on his face as if this were all a misunderstanding that could be easily cleared up between friends. Cristo strode closer to press fingers against the cop's lips.

"There is nothing you can say," Cristo said. "You brought this trouble to my door. That makes this trouble yours."

Tico Ibanez began openly sobbing. One of the shotgun men hooted at this.

"You will take your clothes off." Cristo stepped away, removing his hand from Trabejo's mouth to wipe his fingers on the leg of his jeans.

Under the sentry gaze of the armed men, Levon and the two cops stripped down, tossing their clothing into heaps before them. Trabejo stumbled and fell as he tried to pull his pants off. This amused all but Cristo who stood apart, looking at something on his phone.

Yayo's body was limp and sliding on the dirt as they tugged at his jeans to pull them off. Cristo muttered an order and the chubby man in the red silk shirt crouched by Yayo to break a capsule open under the unconscious man's nose. Levon's 1911 was tucked into the fat man's waistband at the back. Levon could see it as he bent to rouse Yayo.

Yayo stirred, his head jerking upright with a gasp. He was pulled to his feet then, crying out when the raw sole of his injured foot touched the earth. He dropped again to the ground, recoiling into a fetal pose.

"Leave him," Cristo said, momentarily lifting his eyes from the screen on his phone.

Once naked, the three men had their wrists bound once more.

Cristo pocketed his phone and stepped closer to Levon. He studied the scar tissue visible on much of the man's hide. The puckered star-shapes of bullet strikes. The hashmark of white lines that crossed the man's forearms. The zig-zags of shrapnel wounds and signs where the flesh had been severely burned. All of these told a story.

"What agency are you with?" Cristo said. "The DEA? FBI? Maybe you are CIA. You are not Ukrainian. This I know already. So, you will tell me now or tell me later. Now would be best."

"He told you all he knows about me." Levon nodded to Yayo lying in the dust groaning through clenched teeth.

"Is that *all* there is to know, friend?"

"I'm not here on a government operation. This is strictly business."

"Diamonds. Your business is diamonds."

"It's what diamonds can buy me."

"What did you think I would sell to you for diamonds?"

"The name of the man who paid you to take four Curaçao nationals over the border two weeks back."

"And you think I would tell you that for a few *pinche* diamonds?"

"Tell me now or tell me later. Now would be best," Levon said, unsmiling.

Cristo huffed at that, his lips twisting.

"This one has balls," the fatty in red said with a snort.

"Find out how big, Zorro." Cristo gestured toward the hog pens.

Prodded along by the shotgun men, Levon and the two cops moved toward the wooden fence line. The one called Zorro and a second man lifted Yayo under the arms to drag him along between them. Cristo followed, his phone out of his pocket again and his attention absorbed with tabbing at the screen.

They came to a place in the fence that dropped down to waist height for three sections. Through the gap, Levon could see the humped shapes of swine trotting out from under the shadow of the steel roof. Razorbacks and spotted hogs, Berkshires and Yorkshires, a few mixed breeds that looked to be part feral. Some would weigh out at a quarter ton if Levon was any judge of pig flesh. They were consuming machines that could eat a hundred pounds of feed over the course of a day. They would not be discerning in their appetites and chow down on grain, fruit mash, rotten vegetation or flesh with equal relish. Their powerful jaws and razor teeth could chew through bone like it was butter. Stosh Anderson, a kid he grew up with, told Levon once he saw at his uncle's farm a Mulefoot bite through a two-four as if it were a licorice stick.

Corporal Ibanez began shrieking at the sight of the massive animals now crowding the fence. They squealed and grunted, their bodies thumping against the heavy boards of the fencing as maybe forty of them pressed in a close pack. Twitching snouts raised and eyes glassy in the harsh light of pole lamps aimed into the pen.

Levon's interest was focused more on what sat just outside the pen. Mounted on the back of a flatbed Volvo was a large piece of machinery with a conveyor platform that fed into a large engine housing with a gooseneck spout rising from it. The mouth of the snout was suspended directly over the gathering of swine bunched along the fence line. Though the truck it sat on was a rusting hulk resting on dry-rotted tires, the machine was well maintained. Not a hint of rust on the chrome yellow finish that shined in the glare of the overhead lamps. The company name Norcmat in a chrome frame above a set of control levers.

He'd seen machines like this one summer when he hired on to a county crew clearing brush along power line corridors. Though he'd never seen one this size.

It was a log chipper.

"The crybaby first," Cristo said, his eyes fixed on his phone.

The one called Zorro and his equally unattractive

partner hauled the struggling Tico toward the end of the slanted conveyor. One of the men in farmer's overalls turned a switch and the machine came to life with a rumble, a puff of black exhaust belched from a standpipe. The belt began sliding up the conveyor into the mouth of the machine where a drum was turning. The surface of the drum was covered in cone-shaped steel spikes.

"*Espera un momento,*" one of the shotgun men said and pulled a five-gallon plastic barrel from where it rested by the foot of the belt.

He popped the lid and pulled the wooden handle of a brush from the contents slopping within. The corporal fought the grip of the men gripping him as the farmer slopped a generous coat of greasy red goo on him from throat to groin. It smelled heavily of garlic and the cat piss odor of rancid onions.

"Careful with that shit!" Zorro growled, straining to maintain his grip on the slippery Tico while keeping the corporal at arm's length.

"What the fuck, Flaco?" Guapo snarled at a gobbet of the toxic goo landed on the toe of one of his calfskin boots.

"You eat your food without flavoring it?" the farmer said as he ran the brush down Tico's swaying hips. "You think *cerdos* do not taste their food?"

The other shotgun men giggled at this. This was the height of comedy for them.

The man with the tub and brush finished by swabbing a thick load of the sauce on Tico's face. The corporal sputtered and choked while the others expressed their amusement.

"Head or feet?" the farmer with the brush said, turning to his boss.

Cristo flicked his eyes from his phone to say it did not matter.

"Let's see how loud you can scream now, *cabrone*," the farmer said, dropping the brush and bucket to help Zorro and Guapo lift the squirming policeman feet first onto the conveyor.

His hands bound at his back, there was little he could do but rock back and forth as the belt carried him toward the slowly spinning drum in the opening above him. All gathered around to watch the action but for one of the shotgun men who kept his weapon trained on the remaining captives. Cristo also remained apart, his eyes to his phone.

The corporal continued his futile efforts to slow his progress toward the feed end of the machine. He only managed to turn on his side and raise a leg to brace a foot against the safety bar welded in place above the drum mount. It did him little good as he was drawn closer. His howled wordless pleas only served to agitate the waiting hogs to greater squealing, their appetites whetted. From long custom, they knew that these were the sounds that meant a special treat.

Tico's leg muscles strained as he fought to stop his upward slide on the belt. But the sole of his bare foot, slippery with the noxious marinade, slipped off the safety bar. Before he could regain a foothold, his right foot slid within the clutch of the rotating drum. Inexorably trapped, his ankle, calf, and knee were soon in the crushing grip of the drum as he was pulled bodily toward the blades beyond. His animal shrieks drowned out even the high whine of the chipper's five hundred and fifty horsepower engine. His left leg, caught at an increasingly unnatural angle, separated from his pelvis as the base of his thigh bone snapped with a pop like a rifle shot.

Shock set in now and the corporal fell silent as his body slid into the grinding maw of the machine. An arc of pink slurry exploded from the snout end of the discharge spout.

It sprayed down on the massed swine. They snapped and bit at one another in their feeding frenzy to get at the juicy ribbons of raw flesh now raining down on their backs.

And Tico Ibanez was no more.

"Who is next, *jefe*?" the farmer said, lifting his bucket and brush from the ground.

17

Gunny Leffertz said:

"You wonder why I push your ass so hard? It's so you won't fold when the shit's flying."

Las Colinas Sobre El Cenzio Dos

CRISTO GESTURED AT LIEUTENANT TRABEJO.

The cop's fear turned to rage as he was dragged to the conveyor. He called on God and the Virgin to bring down their righteous wrath on all who were here and their children and their children's children. The farmer stuffed the bristles of the brush in his open mouth. He gagged on the viscous sauce running down his throat. The farmer continued down the cop's corpulent body, giving it a good coating of the stuff.

"Head or feet?" the farmer asked.

"Surprise me," Cristo said, his eyes once again on his phone's screen.

It took four of them to haul Trabejo onto the conveyor. They laid him upright where he screamed and thrashed until the moment when his head came under the roller, the skull crushed in a single wet burst. His legs continued kicking for a few seconds as his generous form continued on into the machine. A new shower of flesh and bone fell upon the squealing swine.

"Maybe you are next," the farmer said, walking to Levon with the bucket.

As the chipper rendered its new load to a fine hash, the farmer tilted the bucket to allow a stream of the stinking mess to run down Levon's chest. He painted Levon's face and worked a handful of the mix into Levon's hair. He was pouring the last of the bucket's contents over the seated Yayo when a harsh metallic sound came from within the guts of the machine.

The motor was still running, but the drum had ceased to turn. The clanking sound of struggling gears was joined by a high whining racket of protesting steel. The big engine sputtered and coughed and died with a violent shudder. The farmer rushed to the control panel to turn the power off then leaned over the conveyor platform to see Trabejo's naked calves protruding from beneath the spiked drum. They lay among coils of intestines that had been extruded from the cop's anus by the terrible pressure of the heavy drum.

"What is the trouble, Flaco?" Zorro asked.

"I don't know," the farmer said, genuinely embarrassed. "It is not the machinery. Something has gone wrong."

"The *rurale* was too fat maybe," Guapo offered.

"No. No. The machine's ground men bigger than this

one," the farmer said, turning to the other men in overalls. "Remember that *puerco* last summer? The Guadalupe?"

"Fat like Chatanuga," one of the others called, raising a titter from his compadres.

"More fat!" another barked.

"What's gone wrong, Flaco?" Christo said, pocketing his phone. He held a handkerchief to his nose. The rich stench of fresh offal added to the powerful reek already present.

"I do not know, *jefe*. I maintain this machine with care. This should not have happened."

"You can fix it?"

"If it takes me all night, *jefe*."

"I wanted this business concluded tonight," Christo said. "You are certain you can have this machine working by morning?"

The farmer nodded with enthusiasm.

"Why not just shoot these two and let the pigs do the rest?" Zorro offered.

Christo turned to Levon.

"You know why, don't you, *gabacho*?" he said as he took his phone from his pocket. "I have been texting with some people who know you well. You are an American they very much wish to speak to. They were very displeased when the men they hired did not return. Instead of their men, I can offer you, can't I?"

Christo held the phone up to take a few pictures of Levon's face.

"They will be here sometime tomorrow. They asked that I keep you safe for now. I have a feeling you will wish you had been dinner for the pigs tonight. I fear very little in this life, but I have to confess that the men you have angered give even me an uneasy feeling."

"Did they tell you my name?" Levon said.

Christo's eyes turned skyward as he thought on this.

"Ask Javi Banderas," Levon said.

Christo blinked.

"Ask Fausto Guzman."

El Chistoso and Tio Fausto. Zeta bosses who operated out of Agujereada. Christo knew the names well from stories his mother told. His mother was a Guzman and had cousins in Zacatecas.

"When you ask them, tell them I was at La Yegua on Good Friday."

"Are you fucking with me?" Christo struggled to keep his voice even. "Where did you meet these men?"

"I've never met them."

"How can they know a man they have never met?"

"Because if they met me on Good Friday they'd be dead."

"What is this you are saying?" Christo studied the *gabacho's* face.

He wondered who this man was. He wondered what kind of man could speak with such calm while standing bound and naked among armed men. This man had just seen two men turned to pig feed knowing he was next to join them. Yet, here they were conversing as they might over coffee at one of his *panderias*.

"I might be worth more to the Zacotecas plaza than I would to the guy you were texting," Levon said.

"You think this is a matter of who would pay more?"

"I think it's about who you're more afraid of."

Christo slapped Levon's face with an open palm and again with the back of his hand. Guapo fetched him a bottled water to wash the stinking mess from his hand.

"Put them in the barn and watch them," Christo said, turning to Flaco. "In the morning, we will feed his Mexicano friend to the pigs."

"Where will you be, *jefe*?" Flaco asked as Serpiente and his two bodyguards walked back to their Navigator.

"At my house in town where we will burn these clothes," Christo said with a wave.

"It looks like a *suspensión de la ejecución* for you, *gringo*," Flaco said.

And you, Levon thought to himself as he was prodded toward the largest of the steel buildings. Yayo Lugo had to be drag-carried by two of the men.

18

Madison, Wisconsin

SHE WAS AN UPTALKER. Every sentence rose in tone to form a question.

"I came up to my room, right?" Shoshonna Nixon sat on the edge of her bed in her dorm room clutching a plush of a bright yellow cartoon character. "And I'm shocked, okay? I don't know what to think, right? I'm all like, am I at the right room? Who does this kind of thing, I mean. You know?"

As he made notations in his casebook, Bill Marquez wondered who at the bureau he'd pissed off to get transferred to Hate Crimes.

"This was at what time, Ms. Nixon?" Bill asked, raising his voice to be heard over the buzz of students clucking and tsk-tsking in the hallway.

He'd shut the door to give them privacy but there was no way in hell he was isolating himself with this zaftig, purple-haired nineteen-year-old. His partner, special agent Susan Nomaguchi, was assigned to him as a chaperone. Only she was busy snapping pictures of the swastikas and epithets scrawled on the dorm room door in a, so far, unidentified medium. Bill wished she'd rejoin him.

"Oh, it was like after my first class. Folklore/Music 103." Shoshonna nodded, her maddening lilt made her sound uncertain.

"And at what time did that class end?"

"Nine thirty?"

"And you returned to your dorm room at what time?"

"Oh, as soon as class was over, right?"

"I mean, what is your best guess, Ms. Nixon, of the time at which you arrived at your room?" The little hand is on the...

"I guess it was like close to ten 'cause I stopped on the quad to sign a petition and talk to some girls I usually have lunch with but I couldn't today because—"

"So, approximately ten o'clock this morning or just before."

Shoshonna nodded, black-rimmed lips pressed together, face earnest.

"And the markings on your door were not there when you left this morning?"

She shook her head, violet mane swaying.

"Do you have any idea who might have done this or why?"

"Well, obviously some haters, right?" She sat up straight now, voice adamant, eyes wide. "Some antisemite piece of shit, okay? Someone who hates me because I'm a Jew, you know?"

"Uh huh," Bill said, feigning sympathy.

And it required a professional level of feigning.

"Shoshonna's" legal birth name was Emma Laurel Nixon from Terre Haute, Indiana. She converted to Judaism two weeks into her junior year at the University of Wisconsin. She was about as kosher as a Cajun shrimp boil. Bill knew his statistics on antisemitic hate crimes thanks to the stats from the FBI's Uniform Crime Reporting studies that broke down the crimes by victim as well as nature of the crime from vandalism to threats by phone or mail as well as open assault and arson. One consistent trend in those stats varied little from year to year ever since the stats had been collected. Jews always topped the list, number one with a bullet with the distant second place taken by gay men or lesbian women depending on the year. And in fourth place again and again without fail? White people. But Asian Americans were climbing the charts in recent years.

For real, there were real crimes rooted in real hate. Church burnings, synagogues splashed with pig shit, shootings, beatings, hit and runs all based on race, creed, color, or sexual orientation. But, since he'd been loaned out to the DoJ's Civil Rights Division, he'd come to learn that there was almost always more to the story and that when the perpetrator was brought to justice he seldom turned out to be the image of the unreconstructed, mouth-breathing, bigotry-fueled throwback that was the popular image of the bad actor in cases like this.

When it came to hate, Bill came to realize there was a surprising amount of diversity. It was like everybody hating on everybody. It wasn't just for White folks anymore. Mexicans hated Guatemalans. Blacks hated Koreans. Koreans hated the Japanese. Gays hated lesbians. Lesbians hated gays. And both hated the trans crowd. And there was true equity in the community of Jew-haters. At least that's how it appeared.

And sadly, frustratingly, and with tedious regularity, a lot of these hate crimes proved to be self-inflicted. Either a pathetic attempt to make the victim the center of attention or in order to score political points or both.

Though early in his investigation, Bill strongly suspected that this was the case with Shoshonna nee Emma Laurel.

Early evidence? The girl's rose gold glitter nail polish appeared to be a perfect match for the color of the swastikas and DIE JEW message painted on her doorway. He'd bet the farm that when they dusted the bottle of the same hue that rested on a glass shelf above her vanity that they'd find it mostly empty and bearing only her prints.

The surveillance cameras both inside and outside of Chadbourne Hall would provide further proof. Bill was already girding himself for the tears when they showed this co-ed high-res video of herself carefully painting backward Nazi symbols with the itty-bitty nail brush.

"My parents are probably gonna want me to transfer, you know?" Shoshonna pouted, screaming yellow Capelli half boots swinging above her faux Chippewa woven area rug.

And there the hideously clunky other shoe dropped.

——

THE WEARYING afternoon melted into a disheartening evening and ended with the university agreeing not to press charges against Ms. Nixon and allow herself to quietly return home to the Hoosier State to face the hammer of justice brought down by her own parents over the fifty grand in tuition they'd blown on her.

Bill and SA Nomaguchi nominated to stay at the Comfort Inn in Madison on the bureau's dime rather than face the hours-long drive back to the field office in Milwaukee. Susan went up to her room and Bill treated himself to dinner alone at the Tornado Steakhouse paid for with his own Visa card.

He was well through an eight-ounce filet with sides of garlic potatoes and orange braised asparagus when his phone buzzed in his jacket pocket. It was a call informing him that his time listening to weepy, overgrown adolescents was over. He was no longer on loan to the CRD and was to come back to the bureau for special assignment. In fact, he was to pack his bag and head to the Dane County Regional Airport to be wheels-up for Anchorage, Alaska by midnight. All arrangements had been made and the government jet was fueling up now. This was all told to him by a junior deputy director back in DC.

"Can you give me even a hint about this assignment, sir?" Bill said as he waved his waitress over. "Do you recall the name Levon Cade?" the junior deputy director said.

He did.

19

Nuevo Laredo

IT WAS a condo on Calle Venezuela in a building he owned. It was occupied by a woman he owned.

Cristo ignored her offer to make him dinner though he accepted a cold beer that he drank in the shower. A long, hot shower. He sat in the tub and allowed the jets to strike his shoulders and the nape of his neck.

He sipped the beer.

He thought.

This *gabacho* was troubling. The names he knew. This story of *la yegua*. The mare. What did El Chistoso and Tio Fausto, two *jefes* high above his place in the Zetas cartel have to do with a female horse? Why would they know this man?

It could all be bullshit. The words of a man who might say anything to save himself and his friend. But even in bullshit, there was often a core of truth. And these names were not of men commonly known outside of the *plazas* or law enforcement. There were no *corridas* sung about them.

They were men far above the need for fame or recognition. Dangerous men who let their deeds speak for themselves.

Men who must be approached with care.

Or, Cristo thought as he took a long swig, he could ignore the words of the *gabacho*. He could hand the man over to the men who were arriving the following day. Hand him over and be done with the whole business.

These foreigners were also men not to be fucked with. It would be the smart thing to have done them a favor. It was thinking globally, Cristo decided. His trade extended beyond Nuevo Laredo and the border. The man he spoke to on the phone represented interests on every continent. Getting their hands on this *gabacho* was important to them. They would remember that it was Cristobel Bravo who did this for them.

But then, what were these *extranjeros* to him? Especially compared to the local relationships he had here in Tamaulipas. Even familial relationships, however distant.

He stepped from the shower to towel off. After slipping into a robe, he bundled his clothing in the bathmat and tossed them into the tub. On slippered feet, he stepped from the steaming bathroom into the master bedroom.

It was home to the woman he kept here but was decorated to his masculine tastes. White walls and woodwork trim stained in dark cherry. The barred windows that faced the street were covered in thick red brocade drapes. The walls featured copies of paintings he liked in heavy golden frames. Garish paintings of Aztec warriors either in combat or in the company of nearly naked beauties with manes of flaxen hair.

By the king-sized bed, covered with a real tiger skin, he crouched to move aside a nightstand. A safe was set into the wall behind it. Inside the safe were thick stacks of banded cash in various currencies along with a Chilean passport with his photo but another man's name. There were also three cell phones. He chose the one that was most charged and sat on the edge of the bed to tab in a number.

A child answered, and he asked the little girl to get her father for him.

"My papa is not here," the child said.

"He is there for me," Cristo said with what he hoped was a smile in his voice. "Tell him it is Cristobel from NL."

A man's voice came on the phone then. A gruff voice that sounded as though the owner had been awakened.

"It is late, cousin," the man said.

"And yet your children are awake."

"They are like cats." His cousin chuckled.

"I wouldn't call if it weren't important."

"Then I will call you back." The call ended.

Cristo lay back on the bed. From somewhere in the condo came music and voices from a television. The woman he kept knew when a visit was business and left him alone.

His cell buzzed where it rested on his chest, and he picked it up. A new number with no name assigned.

"What's so important?" the gruff voice said before he could speak a greeting.

"It is about Tio Fausto."

"Yes?"

"There was some business in the past with Javi Banderas. Something to do with a horse."

"These old men and their horses. Always trading them. Always talking of them like they were *vaqueros* in an old movie."

"This was a particular horse. A mare. And something about Good Friday."

There was a long silence on the phone.

"Cousin?" Cristo said.

"Why are you asking about this?" The voice returned; all pretense of warmth gone from it.

"I met a man, a *gabacho*. He knew these names. He

mentioned the horse. He said that Tio and El Chistoso were only alive because they---"

"Who is this man? Where is he now?" His cousin cut him off, the voice of a man fully awake now.

"A *gringo* pretending to be Ukrainian. I don't know his real name."

"Where is he now? Tonight?"

"I have him, cousin. At the pig farm."

"You have him? You are sure?"

"You remember Flaco? He is holding him for me at the farm."

"Get back there, Cristo. Tonight. Do not let this man out of your sight."

Cristo had more questions but the call had ended.

20

Gunny Leffertz said:
"No one lives forever. But only a fool gives up trying."

La Granja

THEY'D BOUND his hands behind him again. Two tie wraps around his wrists. His ankles were bound together as well. They placed him and Yayo in a steel tractor shed against a wall beside a Kubota and a disc tiller. The doors clanged closed leaving them in darkness. Levon heard a chain run through the hasps and a padlock snapped into place.

He waited until the men's voices faded to silence.

"Yayo, you hear me?"

The other man groaned a reply.

"I'm getting us out of here. You hang on."

Yayo muttered something and Levon leaned as close as he could to listen.

"What was that you said, *hermano?*"

"If you're getting up, I'd like an orange soda with lots of ice," Yayo croaked. He made a grimace that was meant to be a grin.

"You in a lot of pain?"

"*Si.*"

"That's good. If your foot hurts, it means you won't lose it."

"Fuck you" was all the other man could manage. Yayo closed his eyes and his head lolled back on the concrete floor. His breathing was shallow but regular.

Levon sat up and began to test the strength of the plastic straps tied around his wrists. They were two bands drawn tight. The first task was to move them from his back to his front. To do this, he'd need to get to his feet.

After sliding his feet toward him, he managed to rise into a crouch after three attempts. He balanced on the balls of his feet, toes spread on the concrete.

He sipped in a lungful of air and took his time letting it out, willing the muscles of his shoulders and back to relax. Inch by inch, he slid his bound hands down his back toward his ass.

Being naked was a bonus. Another favor was the greasy mix of oils and seasonings they'd painted him with. Combined with fresh sweat they provided a lubricant that allowed him to slide his hands and the ties down the small of his back and under his rump.

His shoulder muscles burned with the effort as he pressed his chest into his thighs to make himself as small as possible. He cleared his glutes and sat back on the floor to work his wrists along the back of his legs, straining to bend near double to bring them down his calves and over his ankles and heels and his hands were free before him.

The next trick was the easiest part. The second lesson they taught at SERE school after Lesson One: Don't Get Caught.

With his teeth, he bit down on the tag ends of the ties about his wrists to pull them to their maximum degree of tightness. The tighter the better for what came next.

He raised both hands above his head and brought them down, extending his elbows to either side to use the full array of muscles in his upper body to bring strain to the plastic strips. As he thrust both arms down, he tried to pull his hands apart.

After two tries, one band snapped, the plastic stressed. Two more thrusts and the second band snapped, and his hands were free. Using his teeth, he chewed the stray end of one of the bands thinner. He used this end to slip into the fastener on the ties that bound his ankles. This broke the bite of the fasteners and they easily slid open.

Levon rose to his feet and thought about letting Yayo know he was free. He decided to leave his friend asleep while he searched the interior of the steel shed for anything he could use as a weapon.

The tractor cab yielded nothing. There was a toolbox strapped down to the frame of the disc tiller. Inside, he found a leather-handled hatchet with a rusting blade and a flathead screwdriver. They'd have to do.

He used the flathead to slip off Yayo's tie wraps. The man regained consciousness and tried to speak.

"I'm going out," Levon said, pressing the handle of the screwdriver into Yayo's hand. "But I'm not leaving you. You hear them coming, you put your hands behind your back like you're still trussed up."

Yayo took the tool, nodding.

"*Vaya con dios*," he managed, lying back against the wall.

Levon climbed the tractor to stand on the roof of the cab. From there, he reached up to lay the axe on a roof joist.

He levered himself up onto the joist. Axe in hand, he made his way along the steel joist to where a wall met the roofline. There was an opening there for ventilation. It was just wide enough to allow him through.

He stuck his head out through the vent space. The pole lamp above the pig shed was still lit and there were lights from the windows of another building. The rest of the compound was dark. Shadows moved near the log chipper. One or two men working to find whatever had made it malfunction.

Directly below Levon was an angled rooftop that met the wall of the shed. If he dropped on it the metal would make a hellacious sound. He stuck a leg out into the night and worked his body through the gap until he was hanging down along the wall with one elbow crooked through an upright.

With one hand, he hooked the blade of the hatchet to the top of one of the steel wall panels. He slid his other arm from about the upright and allowed his full weight to dangle from his grip on the hatchet's handle.

The handle, the full length of his arm and his six foot, three inch height, reduced the drop to less than three feet. He'd still make a noise but nowhere near as loud. He'd have to lose the hatchet but there was no help for that. Escape was paramount.

He allowed his sweating hand to slide from the hatchet handle and dropped into a crouch atop the lower roof. From there he slid to the ground. If the noise of his descent raised any alarms then he'd need to move fast.

Hugging the shadows cast by the shed wall, Levon moved toward the light.

21

Gunny Leffertz said:

"If you're given the choice, choose to die last."

The Sty

"*CHINGAR*," Flaco muttered, his arm deep inside an open hatch on the side of the log chipper.

"What is it?" His cousin was steadying the ladder supporting Flaco's weight.

"*Yo no se.*" Flaco tugged at something lodged in the blades within the shaft.

Whatever it was, it had caused the machine to seize. It was metallic and slippery. Flaco braced a hand on the chipper's casing and yanked at the obstruction. It came free with some effort. Flaco held it up in the harsh glare of the pole lamp.

The object was heavy with a ball on one end much like a doorknob and a curved piece of metal that was like a knife blade except that it was rounded with no edge. It was all of one piece and fashioned of metal. Flaco squinted to read a row of letters and numbers imprinted on the blade.

"That was inside the fat cop?" his cousin said from the base of the ladder.

Flaco shrugged and started down the ladder with the mysterious obstruction in the front pouch of his overalls.

In fact, it was a ball joint that Amando Luis Trabejo had implanted in his femur to replace the worn and arthritic hip rotor that had been plaguing him for years. The surgery was performed at a hospital in Tampa, Florida, five years before. It was fashioned from titanium with a silver alloy electroplating. Nothing but the best for the lieutenant.

"Keep your hands where they are." It was a voice that spoke in flat, unaccented Spanish.

Flaco turned in his descent down the ladder to see the naked gabacho standing at the foot of the ladder with a shotgun aimed at the back of his cousin's head. It was his cousin's shotgun, set aside so that the ladder might be steadied.

"Climb down slow," Levon said. "And no talking."

———

THE STORY on the TV made no sense to them. Something about an inheritance and a secret affair many years before. Somebody had fucked someone they should not have and there was a question of legitimacy. It was all confusing.

But the women were beautiful and showed a lot of ample cleavage and so Güero and Primo kept watching. They were nephews of Flaco, his sister's oldest boys.

They shared a blunt and a six-pack, their feet up on a

table in a room that their uncle called his "office." A shotgun lay on the tabletop between their outstretched legs.

Güero turned his head slightly as the door opened behind them. It was Flaco and Beto. They moved stiffly, too close to one another. Güero met his uncle's eyes and saw fear in them. He also saw a third man behind them, his naked skin gleaming crimson in the glare of the pole lamp.

"Tell them not to move," the naked man said.

Güero dove for the Marlin on the tabletop. In his ganja-addled mind, he moved with the speed of a panther. In reality, he moved as if he had all the time in the world.

He did not.

Levon emptied the shotgun into the room. Five rounds of double ought tore men and furniture to pieces.

22

The Slot

"WHAT IS WRONG WITH THE PIGS?" Zorro said as he stepped down from the Lincoln.

"They are hungry," Guapo said.

"They are always hungry. They do not squeal like this."

Cristo opened his door and leaned from the back seat. The Lincoln's fat tires had torn deep gouges in the mud that filled with brown water like miniature rivulets. He looked down to his iguana skin boots with tooled silver tips.

"Tell Flaco I'm here," he said and shut the door of the SUV to seal in the AC and shut out the stink of swine.

Zorro and Guapo walked to the lights of the shed in a series of hobbled hops. Like their boss, neither of them was anxious to ruin another pair of boots in the muck.

Zorro climbed the wooden steps to the deck and pulled open the screen door. He recoiled at the sights and smells within.

The room was a slaughterhouse. What remained of four men lay among the wreckage of furniture, their bodies dotted with white puffs of padding from the exploded upholstery of a sofa. Clouds of flies swirled over a lake of their shared blood. The walls were spattered all around. The room was cast in a pulsating field of red from the patina of blood that coated the TV screen. On the screen, two women were fighting in a restaurant. A real bitch fight with kicking and hair-pulling. Their enraged screams sent a cold thrill of dread up Zorro's spine.

"Get back to the car," he said, turning to Guapo staring open-mouthed in the doorway behind him. "Do it now!"

The screen door slammed shut behind him as he made his way across the room. He had the *gabacho's* pistol drawn in his hand. His boots made obscene squelching noises as the drying blood clung to the soles. Empty twelve-gauge cartridges floated atop the puddle.

The smell was overpowering. The stink of an abattoir with released gasses hanging in the enclosed place like a fog. Zorro pulled up the tail of his silk shirt to hold the hem over his nose and mouth.

It was Flaco and his three men who lay on the floor. That much Zorro could tell by their overalls. There was not much else to identify them. One was missing a head entirely.

He could not find the TV remote among the mess on the floor. A kick from his boot silenced the television. It crashed to the floor; the screen shattered. Another kick opened the *bano* set at the back of the room. Nothing there but a filthy toilet and filthier sink. He was alone with the dead men here.

The pistol raised, he took one last look about the room. His gaze froze on an upright steel cabinet. The doors were pulled open. There was a rifle, an old lever action, with slots for four more weapons. Empty slots. There were rows of ammunition cartons on a shelf above. They had been disturbed. There were gaps in the neatly stacked rows.

He turned to run, slipping in the bloody pool, as he heard the first shot from outside.

Zorro crashed through the screen door and out onto the deck. He saw Gaupo down by the side of the Lincoln, clawing through the muck dragging his legs behind him. A second explosion and Guapo's torso bucked, and he lay still, face down in the shit and mud.

The blast of the invisible rifle echoed off the walls of the compound. Zorro searched for a sign of the shooter's position as he ran for the Lincoln, legs pumping. He placed a hand on the handle of the passenger side door. Something shoved him hard against the door, his head striking the glass.

His legs gave away beneath him. His knees sunk into the mud by the car, his hand still gripping the door handle. There was no pain. Not yet. Only the rhythmic whoosh in his ears responding to the rapid beat of his heart as he tried to make his legs work to lift him upright.

Zorro's fingers went numb and his hand slipped from the door handle to allow him to drop onto his side. He closed his eyes then, thinking that he just needed a moment's rest.

━━━

ZORRO AND GUAPO WERE DEAD.

Cristo watched them die through the tinted glass in the rear of the Lincoln. With sweating hands, he gripped the smooth ivory butt of the automatic he kept in the rear console.

It was a weapon inadequate to the current task. The shooter and he was convinced it was no more than one man, was firing from an elevated position. He sensed this rather than knew it. It seemed to him that his bodyguards were struck down from above.

He began squeezing between the two front seats to drive the SUV away. The keys were in the ignition where Zorro had left them. The engine was running. He tossed the stubby pistol to the passenger seat and maneuvered through the gap in the upright bucket seats.

His knee was on the padded top of the center console when a new shot rang out. A silver hole with a black center appeared in the hood of the Lincoln. Another shot and another hole through the hood. The Lincoln's engine died with a sputter and gasp. The odor of gasoline filled the interior.

Cristo ducked back into the back seat and weighed his dwindling options.

He could make a run for it. Open the right-hand door then throw himself out of the left. The nearest cover seemed so far away. The area around the car was awash in the glare of the pole lamp.

Maybe he could wait here. It was nearly morning. The shooter would be exposed then. Mister Tranh told him his representatives would arrive by noon.

They could deal with this shooter, whoever he was.

And Cristo was certain this shooter was the tall *gabacho*. The *idiota* Flaco had either freed him or allowed him to escape.

His cousin from Agualeguas might be here even before whoever the Chinaman might send. The call with his cousin had ended abruptly and Cristo took that to mean that his cousin would contact El Chistoso. The Zetas would want to talk to this man.

All he had to do was wait in the safety of the car.

If he could.

The heat in the enclosed cab began to rise. The smell of gasoline grew richer. It was giving him a headache. His shirt was soaked through, plastered to his chest and back.

He jumped in his seat as the glass near his head starred.

More beads of glass rained down as he threw himself to the floor of the car. He could feel a draft on the back of his neck.

"Come on out, Snake," a voice called from somewhere outside.

The *gabacho*.

"Guns first." The voice was closer now.

"I have only the one!" Cristo called.

"Let's see it."

On hands and knees, Cristo crawled to the door and pulled the lever. Dawnlight came through the gap in the door. He tossed the pistol out into the light.

"Step out, hands in front of you."

Cristo did as he was told. He stood in the muck with eyes downcast to watch the disgusting muck broach over the instep of his boots.

"Turn around and put your hands on the side of the car."

Cristo leaned against the car, something he had not had to do since he was a young bandito running the streets of NL. In the spider-webbed reflection of the car's glass, he could see a figure separate itself from the shadows. The naked *gabacho*, a rifle held easy in his hands.

"We could have had this talk before," Levon said. "Without all this trouble you brought on yourself."

23

Anchorage

"TAKE HIS CUFFS OFF," Bill Marquez said when the prisoner was brought into the office he was borrowing.

The man was escorted into the room by two local cops. He was maybe the palest man Bill had ever seen. Alabaster white skin and eyes a bleached blue.

"And give him his belt back."

The man booked in as Robert Williams of Louisiana was holding up his pants with one hand as they frog-walked him to the guest chair.

"We're good," Bill said. "Unless you want something."

"I wouldn't mind a coffee and maybe a fried pie or like that," the very white man said with an easy smile.

"Could you help us out?"

"Sure." One of the cops shrugged and closed the door behind him.

"Nice office," the man said, his piggy eyes taking in the window view of snow-covered rooftops.

"It's not mine. The PIO here is out sick."

"You're the fed I asked for." The man's smile grew broader.

"Special agent Marquez." Bill held out the leather folder with his ID card in it. He indicated the phone sitting on the desk between them. "You all right with me recording this?"

"Not till I get a few guarantees."

"Look, I'm gonna be straight with you. You're up shit creek. Your prints came back. I know you're Lewis Dollinger. Former county deputy from Buttfuck, Alabama. You have a history that's sketchy to say the least. Now you're caught dead bang for two homicides."

"You're not from the field office. You said you're a special agent."

Bill said nothing. He waited for where this was going.

"All's I said was 'Levon Cade' and they send you runnin' here all the way from Dee Cee." Lew shifted in his chair to lean on the desk, hands clasped before him.

Bill sat back, taking in Lew's smirk.

"You didn't even have time to change your clothes. Probably shaved on the plane. They fly you all the way here from Washington and you try and act like all I have is nothin'. If that's how you bluff, special agent, then you and me need to play some cards."

"Give me the highlights then," Bill said. "Give me something I can dangle to my section chief."

"That coffee on the way?" Lew sat back.

"Is that how it's gonna be?"

"Baby steps, special agent. That's how we build trust." Lew's eyes crinkled.

Bill had no idea how to use the antiquated phone on the desk. Rows of buttons for different personnel and departments. He rose to go to the door and call out. A female uniform popped out of an adjacent office. He told her to find someone to hustle up coffee for his suspect.

"Don't forget that pie," Lew said, pushing his chair back on its rear legs.

The coffee came along with a Hostess fruit pie from an Alpine Mini-Mart down on the corner.

"I got hired, drafted more like," Lew said around a cheekful of the pie. "Little bitty Asian man travelin' with a pair who look like they came off the Raider's defense line."

"Hired to do what?" Bill dumped creamer from a plastic tub into his own coffee.

"Find Levon Cade."

"And what made them think you could do that?"

"I had a past association with Cade. Let's say our paths crossed."

"I have a feeling you're not going to share the nature of that association."

"Water under the bridge, special agent. Not germane to the matter before us."

"No idea of Cade's whereabouts?"

"Fuck all. You find his girls?"

"His girls?"

"His daughters. You know where they are?" Dollinger's eyes shifted.

"He's only got the one daughter," Bill said.

"He had two in Idaho. You think they're with him?"

"What's *your* interest there?"

"This bunch that's after him. They play hard. I think about those two girls."

"So, you do have a heart."

"Maybe I just come to that part of my life where I'm looking back. You ever look back, special agent?"

"Doesn't everyone?"

"Sure. Only when I look back I don't see much to be proud of. I want to change that."

"Maybe you'll find Jesus when you get to prison."

"He'll have to find *me* first." The smirk returned; the eyes were cold once more.

"Do you have the name of this Asian guy you're talking about?"

"I do not. But I can provide a description."

"A description of an Asian male." Bill raised an eyebrow.

"Yeah. I know. That *is* humorous." Lew brushed flakes of sugar from his shirt front. "Little guy, yay tall. Squinty eyes. Black hair. Talks funny."

"Not very helpful."

"But I can give you a location and a date. A hotel in Florida."

"And what am I supposed to do with that?"

"Come on, special agent. You know there are cameras every-damned-where now. I give you the day and time and name of the hotel and you match my description to the video you pull and run it through those spy programs you have."

"We might be able to work with that. Can you tell me what your Asian guy wanted with Cade?"

"He crossed them somewheres back. I got the distinct impression they want that boy dead. Maybe take a long time killin' him."

"Now *you're* crossing them."

"That's part of the reason we're talkin', special agent. Those guarantees I mentioned."

"Protection."

"To start with." Lew dabbed a gob of apple filling from the corner of his thin lips.

24

La Granja Otra Vez

THE BIG BLACK birds circled in a funnel-shaped cloud that whirled high over the trees that surrounded the pig farm.

Cristobel Bravo's cousin, more like an uncle to him given the difference in their ages, was in the back seat of a Forerunner. He squinted past his driver and bodyguard through the dark glass to see the birds perched atop the roofs of the sty and a steel-walled shack and along the curved neck of a pole lamp. Others squabbled in heaps around a Navigator riddled with bullet holes. The birds swarmed over bodies lying about the vehicle. The sun flashed off their wings in a blue iridescence, their heads wet as they ducked and pulled at the still forms.

He'd driven here from Aqualeguas through the early morning hours. He could not trust such a matter to a grandstanding idiot like Cristo. The bodies now serving as food for the buzzards confirmed his suspicions that his young cousin was into something way over his head.

The carnage here also served to confirm that this man

Cristo claimed to hold captive was one of the gringos from Good Friday on La Yegua. A phantom, a ghost, a creature made of smoke, who was there that night when the heads of a dozen *plazas* were cut off along with high-ranking *jefes* from the three *grande* cartels.

It was a massacre, a reprisal strike from the *Norte Americanos*, unlike anything since the countermeasures taken after the torture-murder of Kiki Camerano. It was not touted as a victory by the *gabachos* in Washington. It was never made public. Nor was it a subject of song or story among the cartels.

They came. They killed. And that was enough. It was clearly meant to strike fear into the narcos, or, at the very least, cause chaos in the ranks. And, it was true, the only outside force the cartels feared was direct military action from the United States. The murder of so many at what was to be a secret conference sent a chill through the chief *narcos*. They were uncertain of their future. They expected this to be just the start of a campaign to bring them down in a series of operations like the ones that had brought the Taliban low.

Yet the real effect of the raid on La Yegua was only to set back business until a new order could arise to run the business of drugs. Scores were settled and the most ruthless stepped forward to take the place of those who died on Good Friday.

And, as always happened, the reins of power shifted in the USA and a new regime came into office with ideas of their own, the same old ideas that had allowed the drug trade at the border to flourish for decades. Capitulation, co-operation and lofty ideals took the place of direct, violent action and the tide of meth, coke, weed, and heroin flowed north in even greater volume than ever before. The lion of the North had roared and then gone back to sleep.

But still, in the backs of the minds of the *veijos*, who were the true masters of the cartels, was the knowledge that the wind could shift again. There could always be more Good Fridays. There could be an *El Norte* that would blow across the border and wipe them all away. But instead of a cold wind gusting south along the Gulf, it could be a storm created by the blades of *Americano* gunships.

And now he had arrived too late to find his young cousin had caged a *tigre* but failed to hold him.

He walked with his men to the Navigator. A lit cigarette in the corner of his mouth more to mask the stink of the sty than from a desire to smoke. A few rounds from their pistols scattered the vultures who rose in a silent cloud to perch atop the ridgelines of the surrounding buildings.

Cristo was only identifiable by his boots and the chain he wore about his neck as his face had mostly been torn away by the curved beaks of the carrion eaters.

"There are more inside, *jefe*," his driver said from the open door of the shack.

"What are we to do with them?" his bodyguard asked.

"There is a tarp in the back of the Toyota," the older man said. "Place my cousin in this. I will see that his mother can bury him properly."

"And the others?"

"Tip them over the fence for the swine. They failed to protect their *jefe*. They deserve only to be shat from a pig's ass for that."

It was in the middle of this unpleasant task that the black car arrived. It crunched to a stop on the gravel before the largest of the shed buildings. It squatted there like a beetle, windows black, engine purring.

The older man, his eyes never leaving the idling Suburban, patted a hand toward his two men. They'd dropped one of the shattered bodies pulled from the shack and drawn their pistols once more. At the order of their *jefe*, the men lowered their weapons to their sides.

The front doors opened, and two large men emerged. They had to be *gringos*. Only *gringos* grew so large. A Black man and a White man in gleaming white dress shirts worn under black body armor. One held a shotgun in his fists. The other, the negro, carried a very large, belt-fed weapon. They stood flanking the still-running Chevy, guns held to their hips while the rear driver's side door opened.

A leg was extended from the door opening. It might have been the leg of a child. The dainty foot was shod in a leather loafer of crocodile hide. Small hands reached from inside to slip a black rubber bootie over first one foot and then the other before the passenger stepped down onto the muddy ground.

It was a tiny Asian man, reed-thin and at eye level with the big SUV's side mirrors. He joined the two big men and standing between them emphasized his diminutive stature.

But Cristobal Bravo's cousin knew that this Chinese, or whatever he was, was the most dangerous of the trio standing before him.

"May we talk?" the little man said in carefully enunciated Spanish.

25

Gunny Leffertz said:

"When the killing's done, the best thing to be is alive. The next best thing is to be gone."

Carretera Federal 281

"YOU'D BETTER GO easy on that," Levon said as he drove.

"After the past few days, I will never go easy on anything as long as I live," Yayo said and took a long drink from the off-brand tequila they'd picked up at an Oxxo north of Falfurrias.

"Be better if you drank some water. Maybe eat something."

Yayo shrugged, his eyelids heavy with exhaustion and drink.

They were driving south in a Ford pickup Levon found

in one of the sheds at the pig farm. They wore overalls scrounged from a laundry shed. Levon got them t-shirts with the Mexican flag on them when he bought the tequila. He also bought them sandals, two jugs of water and some burritos as well as a bottle of Amoxicillin and another of something like Advil. If the young woman at the counter noticed the blood on the bills Levon paid with, she showed no sign.

He washed Yayo's wounded foot as best he could and wrapped it in a couple of the T-shirts as a bandage secured in place with duct tape. The foot was bad but did not show signs of infection. Not yet. He'd need to see a doctor as soon as possible. But not in Tamaulipas. It would have to wait until he was home again in Veracruz. Even then, he would need to see a physician he could trust or pay to be silent.

"My wife is going to be very mad at you," Yayo said. "Mad at me too."

"Show her the money." Levon nodded toward a trash bag that rested on the floor at Yayo's feet.

It was filled with bills, American and Mexican, he'd come across on the same locker where he'd found the Winchester Model 70 that now lay concealed under the seat behind him. A rough count put the amount at over two hundred thousand. Most of it American currency. These plazas were always awash in ready cash.

His Colt automatic lay under his right thigh, retrieved from the dead hand of the man in the red silk shirt.

"They are all dead?" Yayo said, plucking a paper-wrapped burrito from the paper sack that lay between them.

"All of them," Levon said. "There's no one left who saw us in Nuevo Laredo."

"The Snake held out for a while."

"That was regrettable."

"And you got what you came for?"

"I got enough."

"Enough will have to be enough, I guess," Yayo said, looking with disinterest at the cold burrito lying unwrapped on his lap.

Cristobel Bravo told Levon all that he knew after some persuasion. Levon told the truth when he said he regretted it all. It was not a brand of work he liked. No matter that El Serpiente would have seen him and Yayo fed to the pigs. That was business. So was what Levon had to do to get the answers he needed.

This was, all of it, about protecting his girls. The mistakes of his past were meant to stay there. But Bravo's coerced cooperation confirmed what Levon had suspected. The criminal group behind the events back in Maine were the ones stalking him.

A crew of professional thieves had shown up at the lake community where Levon was a caretaker under the name of Mitchell Roeder. They were there to find a cache of jewels, cash, and account files of a fraud artist who'd bilked billions from his unsuspecting victims. It was a hunt that had taken the crew from Bali to backwoods Maine. And all financed by an Asian cartel that wanted their payday, a return on their investment.

As it turned out, the lake house in Bellevue *was* the Aladdin's cave they'd been looking for. It was loaded with a fortune in currency, uncut diamonds and the passcodes to billions of dollars hidden in banks across the world.

In the end, they all turned up dead and Levon turned up with the gems, money, and the flash drive that gave him access to a fortune. It was money enough for him and Merry to run. It allowed them to go home to Alabama and hide in plain sight.

Most of it was gone now. He had to turn the accounts over to the feds to buy himself some peace. The cash he managed to keep went to buy cars and the property in

Idaho he was forced to abandon. His stash was down to the diamonds. And they were buried in a coffee can in the dunes behind Yayo's house. He'd dig them up when he got Yayo home. The trash bag of cash he'd leave with his friend except for the money he'd need to travel.

First out of Mexico and then to Asia.

BOOK II

VIETNAM

1

College Station, Texas

IT WAS GOING to be one of those days.

J. T. Garrett turned onto the lot of the Riverbend Professional Park looking forward to a light workload for a Friday and the three-day weekend to come. To celebrate this happy set of circumstances he bought a large window box of Krispy Kremes on his ride in to share with his staff of ten employees. They sat on the passenger seat of his H3 and he could almost taste the apple crumble cruller he'd picked out for himself.

He pulled up to the front of Lone Star Solutions to find some asshole parked in his reserved spot just to the right of the entrance. A piece of shit minivan with Texas plates and a faded Honk If You Love Cowgirls bumper sticker.

It was just after seven in the morning, the sun barely above the cottonwoods and the parking lot almost empty. No reason on God's green earth anyone needed to take his spot.

He swung the Hummer into the next space and brought

it to an abrupt stop that caused the box of donuts to slide to the floor mat.

"Shit," he hissed as he shouldered his door open.

The driver's side door of the minivan opened as he approached. A tall, rangy bastard stepped out, hands easy at his sides.

"Hey, Tobey."

"Aw, fuck," Garrett said.

"There somewhere near here we could go and talk?" Levon said.

"Fuck," Garrett said.

━━

THEY TOOK a booth away from any windows at an IHOP and ordered coffee for both and country-fried steak and four eggs scrambled for Levon.

"You forget to pay your phone bill?" Garrett said as the waitress hustled away.

"Thought I'd want to look you in the eye this time," Levon said.

"Before or after you fuck me in the ass?"

"I'm in trouble."

"And you look like shit."

It was true. Levon's face had a drawn look that a yellowing bruise on one side of his face did nothing to improve. There were scabbed-over wounds across the knuckles of his hands. The real difference was in his eyes. There was a weariness there that Garrett had never seen before. Not in Fallujah. Not in Tikrit. Not even in the Helmand.

"So, you're in a shitpot of trouble and you want me to climb in beside you," Garrett said, but he was smiling.

"All I need is some intel and some papers."

"Must be a heavy load for you to show up in person."

"I need to leave the country. I need ID that's bulletproof."

"That's a tall order for someone with your history."

"I can pay for it."

"Fuck you, Cade. You running *away* from something or running *to* something?"

"You ever hear of an outfit called the Red House?"

Garrett tapped his spoon on the rim of his coffee mug as he studied Levon in silence.

"They're based out of Vietnam," Levon said to break the silence.

"I know where they're fucking based out of, Cade," Garrett said, receiving a reproving look from the waitress who was setting a plate before Levon.

"I never heard of them before the other day. That means they run a tight operation."

"They're not looking to make the nightly news. No one's making movies about them. They're like shadows on a wall." Garrett watched Levon saw his steak into strips. "What does this have to do with you?"

"I did something to piss them off a few years back."

"Your natural talent. Have they caught up with you or are you trying to get ahead of that?" Garrett already knew the answer. Levon's haggard look told him that much.

"They sniffed me out in Idaho. I had to send my uncle and the girls away. Even I don't know where they are."

"Girls? I thought you only had one daughter."

"Long story."

"None of my business. I get it. What'd you do to them?"

"I took something they think belongs to them."

"And they want it back?"

Levon shrugged.

"Then give it back."

Levon shrugged again.

"It's gone," Garrett sighed. "So, what do you have for me?"

"I have a line on them but it's thin. A few names. That's all I have to go on. I need to know what I'm up against."

"Well, all I know is, they sprang up during the Japanese occupation of Indochina during World War Two. A vacuum was created when the war disrupted the opium trade. These guys jumped in and took over, moneymen who'd been doing business with the French."

"Not a triad then."

"Strictly Viets. They kept the flow of dope going right under the Japaneses' nose. Kept it up under the French then us and the ARVN and right up to today with Ho and his followers in charge. You know what it takes to run a criminal operation in a police state? These guys do not fuck around."

"How do they hide their operations?"

"In broad daylight. I told you they were moneymen going way back. They folded the dope trade into their legit businesses and used the extra capital to expand. They own a bunch of legit businesses including a bank in Kuala Lumpur. You're not going to be able to push these fuckers around even if you could find them."

"Can you work up a file for me?"

"You're going after them? How's that work, brother? They know you and you don't know them. Besides, you'll stick out over there like a drag queen at a bar mitzvah."

"I can't be the only American traveling over there."

"What's the plan? Do you have one?"

"Best scenario? I discourage them from coming for me anymore. Worst case? I draw them away from my family."

"By going samurai."

"I don't see another way," Levon said, wiping at his plate with a wedge of toast.

"It's not like I can talk you out of this, is it?" Garrett sighed again.

Levon's answer was to signal the waitress for the check.

2

Gunny Leffertz said:

"The more you lie, the less you talk."

Detroit To Windsor

CANADIAN CUSTOMS WOULD BE the first test of his new ID.

Levon had been to dozens of countries on five continents. Sometimes legally. Most often not. In his experience, Canada had the most stringent customs he'd ever encountered outside of Israel. But, like any government agency, it depended on whether you ran into a wage drone or a ballbuster.

He chose midmorning on a weekday, counting on the heavy northbound traffic on the Ambassador Bridge to provide cover. A heavy lake-effect sleet wouldn't hurt either.

The signs directed passenger cars and commercial trucks into separate lanes. Levon chose NEXUS lane two and pulled his rental Sierra into line at a booth. The cars before him were waved through, each after a two-minute stop to show documentation.

When his turn came, he knew in an instant he'd pulled a ballbuster. A heavy-set woman in a parka that added to her girth eyed him over the top of cat-eye glasses. The look was deep suspicion mixed with disapproval. She twirled a gloved finger at him.

"Can you cut your engine, sir?"

Levon did as he was told.

"Passport."

He held his passport out to her. She took it from his hand.

"Have you had your vaccinations, sir?"

"Yes," Levon lied.

"Do you have proof of vaccination?"

"I filled out the ARRIVECan app," he said and tabbed his phone to reveal the QR code that assured him smooth passage into the country.

He held the phone out to her, but she barely glanced at it.

"I'm going to need you to restart your car and pull ahead to the customs station."

"Is there a problem?"

"No problem at all, sir," she said with a wincing smile and waved him forward after returning his passport to him.

Beyond the check booth he was directed into a parking slot before a single-story flat-roofed building.

"Leave your keys in the car and step through the doors in front of you," a customs officer in a rain slicker and plastic-covered cap said, stabbing a finger toward the doors.

He joined a line that led to a counter with only one station open despite ten or so uniformed officials milling around or sitting at desks absorbed in whatever was displayed on their monitors. When it was his turn at the window, Levon presented his passport, driver's license, and phone all under the name of Steven Cassell of Lexington, Virginia.

The woman behind the counter reminded him of a pecking hen the way she ducked her head up and down to study his passport photo then look up to examine his face over and over.

"This photo is recent," she said.

It was. The pictures taken for him by Tobey Garrett were meant to reflect his current appearance. His hair trimmed short and his beard grown in.

"My previous passport expired. You can see by the date of issue. I just got this one."

"Um-hm," she said as she held a scanning gun over his phone to register the QR code displayed there.

"So, we're good?" he said.

"Take a seat on the bench to your right. Someone will be out to get you. Next."

She did not return his phone or passport. He took a seat on a bench.

A rail-thin guy in jeans and a CBSA windbreaker came out into the lobby and asked Levon to follow him into a back room. He wore a holstered handgun and pepper spray on his belt. The room was a windowless space with a long Formica-topped table in the center but no chairs. Three men and a woman, also in CBSA windbreakers were waiting inside.

They started by having Levon empty his pockets into a plastic tray. Next, they asked him to remove his coat. His coat was laid on the table and two agents felt the lining looking for whatever they suspected he might be hiding.

Another agent went through his wallet taking out each document, card and receipts that had been placed in there to back up his Steven Cassell identity. Even the wallet was properly time-worn.

All the while the agent in blue jeans asked him questions. Some were standard, and some were leading while a few bordered on rude to confrontational. They were meant to elicit a response. Even a wiseass answer would be enough excuse for these petty tyrants to subject him to further abuses of their authority. A strip search and detainment.

Levon didn't rise to the challenge, keeping his replies to polite, direct answers. He did, without stating so, betray a bit of silent bewilderment at why he was being singled out in this way. To play it too cool would be an indication that he might be someone worthy of further inspection. Better to be the cowed American daytripper who only wanted to get on with his day. Just another sheep.

Frustrated at their efforts to get a rise out of him, they returned his coat and belongings to him, and the female agent showed him to the lobby. Three more agents were completing a search of his Sierra, all doors open. The contents of the front and rear center consoles spread out on the seats. His luggage sat unzipped on the dropped tailgate. One of them was speaking into a handheld radio. He handed Levon his car keys.

"Welcome to Canada, sir," he said with a fixed smile.

———

AFTER A LONG DAY OF DRIVING, he left the Sierra in long-term parking at Toronto Pearson International and took the shuttle to the main terminal. There he checked his bags as Thomas Creighton of Montreal on the Cathay Pacific flight for Hong Kong departing in four hours. He'd already tossed his Steven Cassell ID in a bin at a Tim

Horton's back in Kitchener. His full beard was gone leaving only a neatly trimmed mustache and goatee. A pair of reading glasses helped alter the shape of his face and matched the picture in the Canadian passport Garrett's guy had provided for him.

Once through the long line at customs, which was much less stringent for those leaving Canada, Levon settled into the Cathay Pacific travel lounge for a complimentary coffee or tea. He sipped coffee while pretending to watch CTV News on a big screen that hung over the strip that announced flight departures.

He was among the first to board and was soon stretched out in first class by a fussy Asian man in the window seat who, thankfully, spoke no English. The man played with recharging cables for his tablet when not pestering the first-class attendants with questions in a whiny Cantonese drawl.

Once they'd taken off, Levon gratefully accepted the offer from one of the attendants of a double vodka rocks. She offered him a professional smile that wore away around the edges when she glanced at his troublesome seatmate.

He set the empty glass on his tray table and reclined his seat as the cabin darkened and a movie began on the screen set in the seatback before him. It was something about fast cars and foreign intrigue and played silently as he'd not plugged in his headset. There were subtitles in Chinese.

Levon Cade was soon fast asleep, the vodka helping to still his thoughts and unwind the tension in his shoulders.

3

Anchorage

THE PIG-EYED ALBINO'S lead worked out.

Video from a Marriott in Punta Gordo, Florida, showed a dapper little Asian man accompanied by two men so large he looked like a child being escorted by ogres.

High-def shots from within the window Lewis Dollinger provided showed the trio entering the lobby, in the elevators and in the hallway of the room registered to an alias Dollinger gave up. There were more than enough angles to feed to the lab at Quantico for facial recognition passes.

The reports came back within forty-eight hours and Bill Marquez reviewed them at a table in the break room. The public information officer was back from her bout with the flu and had re-taken her office.

The two goons who'd roughed up Dollinger were ID'd. One of them actually had played a season with the Raiders. Both were domestic talent hired out of a casino in Vegas. Field agents there were running down their local whereabouts.

The diminutive Asian guy was more problematic. It wasn't that the NGI (Next Generation Identification) system couldn't put a name to the face. It had too *many* names for the face.

The guy was either Kam Li Fong, a restaurateur from Marseilles or Stewart Park, a contractor from Seoul, or Prachaya "Pat" Ketukaeo, a hotel owner from Phuket or Bin Liu Tranh, a businessman out of Hue in Vietnam.

The analysts agreed to a ninety-eight percent certainty that the guy on the videos was the same guy and that he matched positively to all those AKAs. A deeper dive with the counter-terrorism people confirmed this. A friend from the Academy, currently in the Bureau's International Operations division, gave him the good, the bad, and ugly, rumor and fact and suppositions on the little man in the shiny suit.

"He's a fixer for a Vietnamese mob," the friend told Bill in a phone call. "He makes problems go away."

"So, which name is the true ID?"

"My guess is Bin Liu Tranh. The dude looks Viet or Laotian."

"So, you can tell each other apart?"

"Fuck you, beaner," Agent Gary Yakahama said before breaking into his unmistakable donkey-bray laugh.

Bill was back on the phone with the biometrics division.

"I have a name and a face, but I need a current location."

"Do you have a city and state?" The voice was cute with a hint of a drawl. Bill wished it was a Zoom call so he could see what she looked like.

"I don't."

"You want an NGI scan of the whole country. This guy planning on blowing up the White House?"

"So, that's out of reach?"

"Maybe if we were on *Star Trek*." She was funny too. The way she said it was dismissive. She wasn't a nerd.

"I could narrow the search a bit. Suggest places to look."

"Okay."

"Idaho, for one."

"The state of Idaho."

"Yeah."

"The whole state?"

"Well, actually Idaho County around a town called Elysium." Bill assumed that Tranh would be following the path from the last place he had contact with Dollinger.

"Well, that can't be too much of an ask. Small town. Only a few cameras, I'd guess."

"And Anchorage, Alaska."

"That where you are now, Agent Marquez?"

"Yeah. And before you ask, it's cold."

She laughed a throaty chuckle before saying, "We'll run the program but I can't promise anything. This system is still in beta no matter what the press releases say."

"Tell me about it. I was on a tactical in New Mexico last year. Facial recognition was dead cert on an ID for a serial bank robber. We bust in like the O.K. Corral and it's a guy who's been in a wheelchair for ten years and never left the state in his life. A reform rabbi to boot."

"Like I said," a smile in her voice. "I can run it but there's no guarantees."

"That's all I can ask," Bill said aloud but thought to himself, "other than your cell number."

———

"YOU GOT YOUR DEAL," Bill said.

"What deal? We ain't even talked about a deal," Lew Dollinger said.

They were in a visitation room at the Anchorage Correctional Complex where they'd stowed Dollinger after his arraignment on two homicides. It was a dreary, windowless room with plastic walls, plastic chairs, and a plastic table. Bill brought him McDonald's.

"Okay, let's hear what you want," Bill shrugged.

"So, everything I told you checked out?"

"It checked. Your lead put us on a Vietnamese national with ties to a big racket in Asia. Far as we can determine, he's still in the US unless he scooted on a charter."

"That Chinaman ain't goin' nowhere, special agent. His job is to find me and find Cade. He ain't goin' back to Vietnam empty-handed." He pronounced it Vee-ET-nam to rhyme with Spam.

"What you gave us is good. But it's no Get Out of Jail Free card."

"Look here," Dollinger grinned as he leaned over the table, gesturing with a McNugget in his greasy fingers. "You can convince these Yukon motherfuckers to reduce the charge to manslaughter with cause. Those boys I capped weren't no Jehovah's Witnesses."

"You gunned them down, Dollinger. Cold blood."

"Before they could gun me down. This is a stand-your-ground state, you know. I was within my rights."

"You've done your homework. I can do what I can to reduce your sentence, but the judge is never going to agree to self-defense. You're not walking."

"Shit."

"You're looking at four to eight. You'll probably wind up doing two."

"I can do that but not here. Not in maximum."

"There's no country clubs anymore."

"Fuck, I know *that*. But you could work minimum security. Someplace warmer."

Bill studied Dollinger's face. The man kept that simple shit-kicker grin fixed on his face, but those piggy eyes were pleading. An ex-cop in a state lock-up would be in constant danger.

Added to that, this Tranh guy had juice. It would be nothing to hire some cons to take care of Dollinger. That would be far less likely in a minimum-security facility where he'd be in with deadbeat dads, drunk drivers and sneak thieves.

"I think I can make that happen. When's your hearing?"

"Next week."

"Plead guilty. I'll have a word with the judge. If we bag Tranh in the meantime, I might be able to work some magic at the bureau, see that you get easy time in a county lock-up in the lower forty-eight."

"You're a prince, special agent."

"Now, if you could hand up Cade too, I could probably get you informant status. You could be out in a month."

"Son, I got no help for you in that direction. That boy is *gone.*"

"Never hurts to ask, as my mom used to say." Bill pushed his chair back and stood.

"You think you're coming back this way, special agent?" Dollinger said, turning to the door, his cheek bulging with fries.

"Could be. Have to see where the trail takes me." Bill stood at the door, knocking for the guard.

"Well, next time could you bring Popeye's?"

4

Gunny Leffertz said:

"The best disguise is looking like you belong right where you are."

Ho Chi Minh City

THE GUY at the rental counter did everything he could to talk Levon out of renting a car. In Viet, French, and finally in tortured English, the guy practically begged him not to do business.

His reasons were many. The traffic in Saigon was horrible. He would get lost. It was the tail end of monsoon season and the rain made driving dangerous. And he had a brother-in-law who would gladly drive Levon anywhere he wanted to go for only two million dong a day.

"I want a car," Levon said in his own mix of English and tourist French.

"*Non. Non.* Is not good. Is not beneficial," the guy said, shaking his head. It came out "ben-EE-fish-ull."

"Big car," Levon insisted, holding his hands apart to indicate size.

The largest he could manage was a Jeep Compass. It was only a few years old and battered as a ball gatherer at a driving range. The driver's seat was sprung, and the gear shift felt like it was connected to a bucket of pasta.

There was no AC. He had to drive with the windows up or get drenched. Two clip-on fans mounted on the dash were his only relief from the suffocating heat trapped inside the SUV. His shirt was soaked through with sweat within thirty seconds.

But the wipers worked and that was most important. The rain came down in a steady stream turning the world gray. Levon could see little past the hood of the Jeep on his drive along the highway from Tan Son Nhat to the city proper. He followed the red lights of the cars and scooters before him. At times, the downpour was intense enough to cause a sense of vertigo. Only the frequent ruts and potholes in the road surface let him know he was moving at all as he couldn't hear the engine over the hammering of the rain on the hood and roof.

By the time he found his hotel an hour later, he was sure he knew what pilots experienced when flying on instruments only. His only guide was the Avenooz app installed on his phone to tell him when to turn and when to come to a stop. The calm feminine voice instructed him around the traffic circles packed with speeding bikes and scooters all bleating their horns at him as he shifted lanes to find his way off the roundabouts.

The pounding on the roof of the Jeep was silenced as he pulled beneath the portico of the Sofitel Saigon Plaza. A valet greeted him with a hand out. Levon dropped the keys of the rental in his hand and the valet's grin vanished. Levon fished in a pocket and peeled a US twenty off a mixed roll of dollars and dongs. The grin returned, and the valet handed him half a yellow ticket.

Levon barely had time to lift his bags from the hatchback before the valet tore off into the deluge, horn blasting to make a gap in the traffic. He wondered if he'd ever see the rental again.

The air conditioning in the lobby felt like an arctic blast after the stifling humidity outside. He made his way to the registry desk to claim the single room booked under the name Thomas Creighton. The smiling man at the desk asked way too many questions as he made a copy of Levon's driver's license and the photo page of his passport. His answers were vague as the man quizzed him in French and Levon couldn't understand about half of what the man was asking him.

He offered a MasterCard and signed for incidentals. A porter in a white mess jacket appeared to carry his bags to the elevator. The porter didn't ask any questions and remained glumly silent during their ride to the sixth floor. Levon decided that he liked this guy. He tipped him a half million dong once they were in the room. That brought out a wincing smile from the porter and a few genial words in Viet as he bowed himself out into the hallway.

Levon stripped off his clothes and took a long, cool shower. He reset the shower to a hot blast and sat cross-legged on the tiles to allow the stream to strike his neck and shoulders. His muscles were stiff after nearly a day and half of air travel. He stood and turned the tap to cold before stepping out to towel off.

Naked, he stood before the window of the room and looked out through the water-streaked glass at a dismal monochrome world. Neon signs glowed faintly through the monsoon haze as afternoon gave way to evening. The signs winked and cascaded, appearing to hover in the air unsupported as even the buildings across the street were invisible in the heavy torrent.

He lay down atop the covers by his unopened bags and was soon in a deep sleep.

THE RAIN HAD DIED AWAY to a light drizzle the following morning. The heavier showers the day before did nothing to tamp down the crushing humidity in the air. It felt to Levon as though he was breathing through a straw as he waited under the portico for the valet to bring his Jeep around.

He entered traffic with his windows rolled partly down and the fans on high. The Avenooz voice informed him that his destination was twenty minutes away on a road called Luy Ban Bich.

The narrow street that ran before the hotel gave way to a wider four-lane entered through one of the maddening roundabouts that seemed to be located everywhere across Saigon.

That was one of the first things he noticed as he drove. Though on maps and in his travel itinerary, the city was always referred to as Ho Chi Minh City, all of the signage on storefronts and the sides of buses proclaimed the place to be Saigon.

The traffic was denser than the night before. Or maybe it only seemed so because he could see it now in the watery sunlight trying to break through the overcast. Every lane was clustered with motorbikes, scooters and e-bikes often with two or more riders. There were cars and jitneys and pedicabs all weaving and crowding and fighting for space on the roadway. Massive behemoth tour buses made their way through the crush like whales through schools of cod.

And all of these vehicles had one thing in common. They were all honking and beeping at Levon. Or at least that's the way it felt.

His promised twenty-minute ride turned to thirty, then forty as he missed turns and had to do more than a few circuits around the three circles he came across. He pulled up to a gate in a cyclone fence that ran along one side of the lot where DannCo Stylewear sat. The fence was topped with loops of razor wire. A Viet in a short-sleeved uniform shirt stepped out of a booth to glance at his open passport before sliding the gate aside and waving him in.

DannCo was housed in a steel-sided warehouse building showing signs of rust where the panels of beige siding joined. The sign mounted above the entrance was new.

Levon pulled into the nearest available spot and walked between rows of Toyotas and Nissans. There was a Mercedes sedan parked by a Lexus in the reserved spots near the entrance.

Entering the building was like stepping onto another planet. The high-ceilinged lobby was brightly lit by suspended fixtures. The floor was polished terrazzo. A fountain gurgled in the center of a waiting area accented with upholstered chairs. A pair of attractive Asian ladies sat behind a long reception counter beneath a row of enlarged photographs of skinny models dressed in DannCo's latest offering.

The air in the lobby turned his sodden shirt to ice. He'd elected to wear a light sport coat over an open dress shirt, the common costume of foreigners doing business in the tropics. Or so he'd imagined. Most of the employees he saw arriving for work wore polo shirts over cargo shorts for the most part.

He asked for Carl Winninger at the desk and was invited

to take a seat while one of the girls spoke into a phone to tell someone that Mr.Winninger's guest had arrived. WEEN-in-jer.

Carl Winninger turned out to be a forty-something White guy a few inches shorter than Levon. He strode out into the lobby in a crisply pressed oxford shirt and cotton trousers. His hair was graying at the temples, but he had the bounce of a man who plays a lot of tennis to stay fit. His smile was cool and never reached his eyes as he held out a hand to Levon.

"Thomas Creighton," Winninger said. "We have a few mutual friends, I hear."

"Our circles intersect here and there," Levon said, taking his hand back after a brief, tepid clasp from the other man.

"Let's find a conference room and get you something cool to drink," Winninger said and led the way from the lobby.

"I'd appreciate that," Levon said and followed.

The other man led him along a corridor lined with office doors on one side and curtain wall on the other beyond which lay a dozen or so cubicles where mostly Anglo men spoke on telephones or tapped at computers. Winninger kept up a spate of small talk and polite queries about Levon's travel experience and the weather and suggestions of good places to eat in Saigon.

Their route took them to the rear of the building and a cavernous warehouse space with row after row of workstations where mostly women worked at sewing machines. They were under the supervision of Asian men who strode the aisles keeping a watchful eye. Rack after rack hung with finished capri pants in a variety of sizes and pastel colors. The persistent tapping of the machines was deafening and both workers and bosses wore protective headgear. Levon and Winninger moved between the aisles like ghosts, no one acknowledging their presence.

They came at last to a windowless room whose only feature was a plain, Formica-topped table and two straight-backed chairs. The walls were paneled in acoustic tile as was the ceiling and Levon noted that the room was entirely bereft of any kind of electrical device. In fact, there were not even outlets set in any of the walls.

Winninger's entire demeanor changed once the door to the room was securely shut and locked.

"What the fuck did I do to get saddled with you?" he asked as Levon took a seat at the table.

5

Gunny Leffertz said:

"Only tell the truth when it benefits you. And only just enough truth to get by. The rest of the time you lie like a motherfucker that believes his own lies."

Dannco Stylewear

"THIS IS A CLEAN ROOM," Winninger said, remaining standing, leaning against the door, arms folded. "It's a requirement for doing business in a police state."

"The world is a police state," Levon said with a shrug.

"I'm glad you understand that. I appreciate that you know how much *deep* shit you could get me in if you go cowboy here."

"I just need the cover for a week, maybe. I'm a consultant you hired out of Canada."

"My ass. You're about as Canadian as greens and blackeye peas."

"You owe Garrett, and he owes me. Letting me work out of here is part of the payoff."

"How much did he tell you?" Winninger said, eyes narrowing.

"Just that you got in a jam back when he was with the agency. He poured oil on the waters for you. Let you keep doing business in Asia."

"Well, just to lay it out in plain English for you, 'Creighton.'" Winninger leaned with fists on the tabletop. Levon saw the ring on his left hand. He was mildly surprised Winninger hadn't already worked being a Harvard grad into the conversation.

"I'm prepared to do the absolute minimum for you," Winninger continued. "You can show up here as part of your playacting. But I'm not going to help you do anything that brings DannCo to the attention of the *Bộ Công an.*"

The Viet secret police agency.

"I don't want their attention any more than you do," Levon said, meeting the other man's eyes. "But I'm gonna need more than just setting up house here."

"Like what?"

"Like anything you can tell me about Benny Hung. And whatever you know about Khuat World Industries."

The Harvard man blanched at the mention of the two names. He pulled out a chair and took a seat opposite Levon. He leaned close, voice low and with an edge to it.

"*That's* what you're here for?" he said in a near whisper. "Benny Hung? Why not just go down to People's Square and steal the statue of Uncle Ho while you're at it?"

"Is Hung a public figure here or a private citizen?" Levon said. "There's only so much I could Google."

"Google." Winninger's mouth went slack.

"It's a simple question."

"Is it? Shit, you don't even know where you *are*."

"So, tell me."

"Hung's a number one gangster. Rumor is he's the top man in the Red House. And the red part has nothing to do with communism. It's the color your house will be if you fuck with these guys. They're not ideological. It's money and more money to them."

"I know that part. How do they operate in this environment?"

"It's not like back home. There's no barrier here between crime and politics."

"Like Mexico."

"That's a recent development," Winninger said, his icy demeanor thawing as he warmed to his subject. "We're talking relationships going back centuries here. Red House supplanted the Chinese triads that used to call the shots here. In that way, they're nationalists. And they're not particular about what flag is flying."

"Why would Hanoi tolerate them?"

"When the North took over the show back in '75, that wasn't the end of politics here. Sure, their 'free' elections are fixed up the yin-yang. But there's still a struggle for power and, even here, politics is still about cash."

"And Red House has the cash."

"Right. So, as long as there's not shoot-outs in the street and the majority of the heroin is for export, the Central Committee says, 'play ball.'"

"Then there's no muscle-flexing here in country?"

"That was all settled way back. When the commies were re-educating the masses, the Red House used that time to settle old scores. Once all the right people were dead it was Ho in charge of the government and Red House running the rackets. From then to now, they wash their dirty laundry outside of Vietnam."

"They're hiding in plain sight then."

"All their home-held businesses are legit as far as anyone knows. KWI owns about twenty super cargo ships. They have subsidiaries in construction, hotels, engineering, and manufacturing all over the Pacific Rim."

"And Hung? What's his status?"

"He's a public figure, I guess. You might see him at a rally for the party's favorite candidate. *Singapore Business Review* did a write-up on him about ten years ago."

"Were there photos?" Levon asked.

"Hold on one fucking minute." Winninger's hands turned to fists on the tabletop. "Are you hunting this guy?"

"It's better you not know."

"That's my answer, isn't it? You're not here because any agency sent you. You're here for blood." Winninger pushed himself from the table and stood.

"I'll be gone this time next week," Levon said.

"You'll be dead this time next week. And I'll have the BCA up my ass wanting to know how I know you."

"You were a victim of fraud. A fox got in your henhouse."

"And how the fuck do I make them believe that?"

"Write a check for one hundred million dong," Levon said and placed a business card on the table. "Make it out to Blue Mountain Practical."

"And that's you?"

"It's a shell set up in the Turks and Caicos." Levon shrugged. "Even a lazy investigation will reveal it's a paper tiger. All hat and no cattle."

"And what do you do with the money?" Winninger said, his eyes wide and head shaking as though palsied.

"I use it to finance my trip here."

"So, I pay you to fuck me?"

"You're paying back J.T. Once I'm gone—"

"Or dead."

"—you're paid up in full."

"Jesus," Winninger breathed. "What's he owe you for?"

"Just his life," Levon said.

With a heavy sigh, Winninger retook his seat.

"What do you need to know?"

6

Gunny Leffertz said:

"Walk like you got nowhere to be. Look at nothing but see everything."

Bui Vien

IT TRANSLATED TO WALKING STREET.

Miles of clubs, bars, shops, and vendors set up either side of a narrow street packed with locals, tourists and visiting businessmen. All lit by the garish glow of neon signage and trim. Young couples wearing backpacks, packs of single guys on the prowl, older folks holding their phones out in front of them as they strolled.

Barkers with bullhorns called out in multiple languages over music blasting from speakers mounted in front of the strip joints to create a cacophony of competing beats and voices.

Levon decided to join the nighttime crush for two reasons. He needed to eat, and he needed to know if there was any interest in him. After leaving DannCo, he kept a wary eye on his six o'clock to look for anyone following him. It stood to reason there would be eyes on foreign-owned businesses. It was more than possible that his visit might raise curiosity about him. The streets crowded with bikes and scooters made it nearly impossible to spot a tail. It would be easier to determine if he were being surveilled on the ground, walking.

He had a *banh mi* of shredded pork bought from a street vendor. He took a seat on a steel bench and ate the pressed sandwich as he watched the parade pass by. His clothing was protective coloration. A faded Canadiens T-shirt he bought at a thrift store back in Windsor. Khaki pants and brand new white New Balances. A Blue Jays cap worn low over his brow.

Appearing to be interested in watching bikini-clad dancers in the windows of a club called *Le Chez Vou*, he eyed the street to see if anyone was lingering or stealing glances his way. Levon looked for the telltale bulges of guns or radios under guayaberas and aloha shirts worn untucked. From under the curved bill of his cap, he studied faces, committing them to memory in case they appeared again during his walk.

He finished his sandwich and iced coffee and continued on, keeping pace with the throng, watching his wake in the reflection of the glass storefronts. After a half mile or so, he decided that there was no one minding him.

As he turned to walk back the way he came, the sky opened up. The rain fell in a steady gush, pounding off awnings and marquees to drown out the music. Tourists shrieked with laughter as they ran for the cover of club entrances and shops. It was pointless as all were thoroughly soaked within seconds. Locals and more experienced travelers opened umbrellas, the patter of drops adding to the white noise that blanketed the street.

Levon walked through the spray, hands in pockets and shoulders hunched. He shouldered his way under the shifting canopy of umbrellas. The street was awash in the reflected neon colors from the signs that hissed and popped above. The gutters ran with a rapid stream carrying plastic cups and wrappers along to where grates overflowed to create temporary lakes at each intersection.

Leaving Walking Street behind, he made his way along darker streets lit only sporadically by shimmering street-lamps and the lights of the occasional restaurant or store still open at that hour. The traffic had died down as scooters and motorbikes left the roadways to bus and car traffic. After a few turns, he came to a traffic circle joined by Pham Hong Thai, a broad six-lane avenue.

Pedestrians were on their own in Saigon. Darwinism came into play for anyone trying to cross a street. The trick was, as Levon had learned from observing locals, to just keep moving; set a pace and never stop, slow down or try to run. Drivers would swerve to avoid you as long as you kept to a steady rate of progress.

He crossed the westbound lanes and onto the walkway that crossed the landscaped center of the roundabout. As he moved toward the eastbound lane, he heard the whine of motorbikes behind him. A trio of them, two with tandem riders, came around the curve to cross before him. They were all helmeted, black visors down. They picked up speed to make another turn around the roundabout, their motors rising to a howl as they accelerated.

Levon was at the center of the roadway when the three bikes came full circle, slowing to lean into the curve. They gunned, swerving to pass before and behind him. One of the riders, clinging to the waist of the driver, leaned out with a ball bat held low in his fist. The tip of it scraped the asphalt as the bike canted into its turn.

Levon sidestepped the blow intended for his knee and reached, fingers held rigid. His forearm caught the batter under the helmet. clotheslining the rider out of the saddle to tumble to the street. The aluminum bat clattered to the road surface.

Two of the bikes came to a slewing halt while the third continued its circuit around. Car horns bleated as they jinked to miss both Levon and the stalled bikes. An Audi failed to see the fallen rider and drove over him without slowing.

The remaining bitch rider leaped to the street to rush toward Levon while the others swarmed forward. The one on foot flung out a hand to extend a three-foot telescoping baton.

Levon narrowly dodged a speeding Celica to reach the curb where the ball bat had come to rest. He scooped it up in time to meet the charge of the baton wielder. Leaping aside to avoid one of the bikes, Levon took a glancing blow to the shoulder from the baton. He batted aside the follow-up backhand and drove the blunt end of the bat into the baton man's gut. The man went down, folded in two.

The bikes, all three now, had turned to ride straight at him. Levon backed up on the sidewalk, bat in hands, to meet the lead rider leaping the curb for him. He feinted left before stepping right and swinging the bat to take the rider full in the head. The strike was hard enough to crack the crown of the fiberglass helmet. The rider and bike went in two different directions, the rider falling to the sidewalk in a heap as the bike careened into a steel railing set around a decorative kapok tree.

The remaining riders skidded sideways in order to change course. They joined the eastward flow of traffic around the circle and were out of sight among the red lights heading away along the Pham Hong Thai.

The first rider, the ball bat wielder, lay where he'd fallen, cars brushing past, the occasional wheel running over an already shattered arm or leg. The second, nursing a bruised gut, stumbled away into the hedges at the center of the roundabout. The last lay still on the sidewalk, one unblinking eye visible through the crack in his visor. His bike lay, wheels still spinning, against the dented railing.

Levon wiped the grip of the bat on the tail of his T-shirt and tossed it onto the grass that grew along the verge of the road. The traffic was not slowing. He heard no sirens approaching. Other pedestrians, huddled under umbrellas, stepped around the corpse in the road as they made their way across the roundabout at their deliberate pace.

Pulling his Blue Jays cap lower, Levon continued on to the Sofitel.

———

HE SLEPT LIGHTER than usual that night. He expected a knock at his hotel room door. He anticipated spending the rest of the new day answering questions in some sweaty police station.

The night went by without event, and he woke well before dawn with his right wrist swollen where his arm had impacted the batman. He watched TV as he iced the arm with cubes from an icemaker in the hall.

Cheery, chirpy newsreaders prattled away on colorful, sunlit sets while words in the peculiar Viet alphabet crawled by beneath. Children sang at a school. A pair of tiger cubs were born at the zoo. A man proudly spoke of the roses he'd grown in his garden. A pair of soldiers helped an old woman find her her lost dog.

No stories of two men dying on the Pham Hong Thai

last night. In fact, there was nothing resembling any kind of bad news on any of the channels he flipped through.

Levon was certain that this was just a random robbery attempt. The research he'd done, countless numbers of tourist videos about visiting Vietnam on YouTube, assured him that this kind of street crime was common. Travelers were warned not to carry a bag or camera or wear jewelry like rings, watches or chains. Also, to keep cell phones pocketed and only to carry as much cash as you'd need for the day and to secure that in a money belt or front pocket.

Given the prevalence of street muggings aimed at tourists, the local cops probably weren't all that troubled by some foreigner handling matters on his own. Unless Levon went to the station and reported it, they'd probably be just as happy to write it off as a road accident. Why bring up unnecessary unpleasantness?

Before retrieving his car from the valet, Levon walked to a pharma just down from the hotel and bought a roll of the equivalent of an Ace bandage. Waiting for his breakfast to come in the lobby restaurant, he wrapped the wrist tight before swallowing three Advil with his coffee. He thought about looking through the newspaper that waited for him at his table. But he'd never be able to make heads or tails out of any of it and doubted that a foiled smash and grab would rate coverage anyway.

The valet brought his Jeep around and flashed a smile at the fresh twenty Levon handed him. The rain was back after a sunny start to the day and teemed off the hood and roof as he pulled from beneath the hotel's portico and into the stream of early morning traffic.

It was time to get to work. Carl Winninger had given him a place to start. He'd see where it led.

7

Gunny Leffertz said:

"Be kind to everyone you meet but have a plan on how to kill them."

Khuat World Industries

THE RAIN WASN'T GOING to let up anytime soon. That was an asset as it provided cover for Levon's surveillance of Khuat World Industries corporate headquarters. It was a ten-story high rise at the western edge of District Seven, a suburb of the city and far from the traffic and smog.

Levon sat in his rental, engine off and windows cracked, and watched the front entrance of the building through rain-streaked windows. He sipped from a steel Yeti cup of strong Viet coffee, syrupy and near to espresso in caffeine levels. It would keep his eyes open.

The building was a faceless, featureless façade of glass and steel around a standard block-like structure sitting on forty acres. Through the gaps in the iron fence that surrounded the property, Levon glimpsed the rows of manicured trees that lined strips in the parking lot.

Buses arrived to drop passengers off at a covered stop directly across the street from the building's gate. There was a security booth set by the broad opening in the fence, but it all seemed precursory with the uniformed guard simply waving at workers arriving on foot and by bike. Only a few cars came through the checkpoint, and these were all German and Japanese sedans. Upscale models but nothing as ostentatious as a player like Benny Hung might drive.

This was just one of the facilities owned by KWI and as good a starting point as any. The company owned a half dozen other buildings in and around Saigon. Two pharmaceutical plants, an industrial laundry, and several warehouses along the river piers. There were even more holdings owned through the list of known shell companies Carl Winninger had provided. Though it was unlikely that Hung would ever visit any of these in person.

The monsoon let up momentarily, dying away to a constant light spray. The twilight paled a bit as the overcast above frayed to allow a bit of glare through. The guard trotted from the cover of his booth to draw the gate closed as the last of the day shift arrived.

Levon took another sip and settled back to give it another hour. No reason for the boss man to arrive at the start of the day. Chances were still good a limo or a Tesla would be pulling up. He turned his eyes from the guard seated in his open booth flipping through a manga to watch scooters putt-putt by.

That's when he spotted the girl on the bench under the cover of the bus stop. He hadn't noticed her before.

Everyone who got off at this stop crossed the street to head directly into KWI. He hadn't noticed anyone walk past him.

She was Asian and wearing a shiny yellow raincoat. Blunt-cut raven hair fell to narrow shoulders. Bare legs ended in rubber rain boots that matched her coat. She was transfixed by her phone, or at least appeared to be. It looked as though she was waiting for a ride though a bus came to a stop with a hiss, its doors opening, and she waved it politely away, her head shaking. As it departed, she returned her attention to the phone in her hands.

Twenty minutes passed, and a BMW pulled to the entrance and the guard hopped from his stool to push the gate wide. He showed some degree of deference to the driver but not, Levon judged, as much as would be due a VIP of Benny Hung's level. The guard drew the gate closed and returned to the cover of his booth after the car had pulled through.

Levon turned his gaze toward the girl in the yellow raincoat in time to see her lowering her phone back to her lap. She had been aiming the phone at the gate and stopped when the car was out of sight. He continued watching her as she returned to whatever was holding her attention on the little screen.

The downpour increased with a sudden gush, turning the sky to dusk once more. The view through his windshield vanished under the cascade. Visibility was near zero but he'd be able to see the head or tail lights of any vehicle that approached the gate.

A bus rumbled past causing his rental to shimmy. He watched through the curtain of water running down his windshield at the banks of brake lights came on momentarily as the bus rolled to a stop. The lights dimmed, and the bus left the stop once more.

Levon turned the key to allow the electrics back on and turned the lever to set the wipers in motion. The girl in the yellow raincoat was still there. Still seated on the bench and studying her phone. He turned the key back and the world outside turned an opaque gray.

He returned to watching the gate, or the approximate location of the gate, invisible now through the haze of falling water. There was nothing to distract him and the discordant drumbeat of rain on the roof. The amorphous murk outside reduced his field of vision to the interior of the car. As much as he resisted, his thoughts wandered from the task at hand.

He imagined the girls wherever they might be. At his insistence, Uncle Fern gave no hint of where they'd take off to. He'd given them most of his remaining money cache and it should last them well into next year. Two to three years if they were careful. In his wandering mind's eye, he saw Merry and Hope on a sunlit beach or walking a forest trail to a remote cabin. He pictured them asleep in their beds with Fern snoring in an armchair in front of a television. He could see the three of them together eating in a booth at a restaurant.

Never much for praying, he allowed his eyes to close and offered a silent request that they be safe. He asked for strength and guidance as well. He sought a dispensation, or at least an understanding, for what he'd come here to do. If men had to die, if he had to die, to keep the girls from reprisal for his actions then he hoped God saw that as a righteous mission. Maybe even a form of atonement.

He reopened his eyes at a new sound that cut through the percussion of the rain. A regular tapping on the passenger side window. He tabbed the button and the window slid open. It was the girl in the yellow raincoat, her hood drawn up and dripping as she leaned into the car.

"Who're you working for?" she asked in American-accented English.

8

Gunny Leffertz said:

"Any intel is good intel. Doesn't matter if it's from a friend, an enemy."

District Seven

SHE INTRODUCED herself as Kate Nhan. She pulled back her hood as she took a seat inside the Jeep. Levon could see now that she wasn't as young as she'd appeared at a distance. Not a girl but a more mature late twenties, gone from cute to pretty as the baby fat had left her features.

"Who said I'm working for anyone?" Levon said, offering a roll of paper towels to dry her face.

"You've been sitting here for close to two hours," she said, dabbing at her brow and the backs of her hands.

"So have you."

"I saw you turn on your wipers to check me out."

"I was wondering why your bus was so late."

"You keep trying to change the subject," she regarded him with a crooked smile. "Okay, I'll show you mine first."

He turned away at that, and she offered a dry chuckle.

"I freelance for hedge companies," she began. "Some back in the states and a French company. You'd be surprised what they'll pay for. They can make a lot out of the tiniest bit of information."

"Like everyone showing up for work on time?"

"More like how *many* show up," she said. "You have any more of that coffee? No? Anyhoo, I watch things like work attendance at factories, businesses. Low numbers might mean there were lay-offs, less activity, lower production. Higher numbers mean an increase in sales, a big change or even maybe a new line being produced."

"And someone will pay for that?"

"Sure. Things like that are tells, leading indicators. Cause and effect. It all goes into the analysis. Risk assessment. Should the people who hire me buy or sell or stay put. I can provide data days, even weeks before the media reports it if they report it at all."

"Makes sense. Not a job I'd have ever thought of."

"So, what's your story? Hell, what's your name?"

"Tom Creighton. I'm working for a Canadian company that does business here."

"Bullshit," she said with a broad grin. "What *part* of Canada you from? Nashville or Little Rock?"

"Alabama, actually."

"Roll Tide," she said. "And is that even your real name?"

"For now," Levon said.

"And what business are you in, Tom of Alabama?"

"Wholesale women's casual wear."

"With *those* hands?" she tittered, nodding at his scarred knuckles atop the steering wheel.

He shrugged.

"That's one business that KWI's *not* in, Tom. Why don't you tell me why you're here? There's no *way* you're a journalist. You don't *look* like you're from the embassy." She was discounting him as a spy.

"Let's just say I have an interest in Khuat's CEO."

"Benny Hung?" Her smile faded.

"I'd like to meet him."

"Like, you're a *fan* or something? Like you thought you'd hang out by the gate until his car pulled up and ask for his autograph?"

"More like a business proposition."

"Well, he's a tough sell," she said, eyes narrowing in a new appraisal of him. "Besides, you'd never catch him that way."

"Why not? He works from home?"

"No," she said, rainwater spraying from her bangs as she shook her head. "It's raining. He only commutes by helicopter."

———

"THERE'S a lot of rumors about Benny Hung," Kate said as she sprinkled hot sauce on the seafood rice bowl she'd ordered. "But I guess you've heard them all."

"A few," Levon said, seated across from her in a booth in a loud restaurant packed with tourists ordering from an unfamiliar menu board in a melange of languages.

He was about to dip the corner of a triangular puff pastry into his coffee. She reached a hand over the table to stop him. Levon looked up, surprised.

"That's not a turnover, Tom," she smirked.

"No?"

"It's *banh pate so*. It'll be curried chicken liver or pork with black fungus."

"Okay," he said and took a bite. "So, not sweet."

"Too hot for you?"

He answered her by taking an amber bottle of sauce from a wire rack at the end of the table and dousing the pastry before taking a larger bite.

"You're ex-military," she decided as she sat back. "You guys drown your food in that shit."

"Only way to choke it down sometimes." He tossed the last bit into his mouth, followed by a swig of coffee.

"I'm not going to get a lot of answers out of you, am I?" Kate said, stirring her own iced coffee.

"What brought you back here? You weren't born here." He picked up another pastry, breaking it over a bowl of yellow rice.

"My parents were. They came over in '75. Boat people. They met at a refugee camp on Guam and got married there. Learned English and got all the way to Philadelphia where they both worked cleaning office buildings for minimum wage."

"It took money to get to the United States after Saigon fell."

"You're right. The more money you had the further you got. My grandfather owned a medical supply house here in Saigon. He sold everything to get my dad and my aunts out."

"What happened to your grandfather?"

"My mom and dad bought a dry-cleaning business. It took five years of sleeping in the back of the store and living on beans and rice, but they got my grandparents out. Except my mom's dad. He died during 'de-urbanization.' Still, it's a miracle any of them made it out. They winded up owning six cleaners and moving us out to the suburbs."

"How did they manage that working for minimum wage?"

"Ever hear of the Canal Boys?"

Levon shook his head, his mouth full of *banh so*.

"A Vietnamese gang. A lot of former ARVN. They'd lend money to immigrants."

"Your mother and father took a risk."

"Bet your ass. Those guys had a motto. 'Born to kill.' But Mom and Dad paid back every cent."

"They're lucky. Guys like that don't always let go that easy."

"Guys like Benny Hung?" She was eyeing him across the table, the tilted smile reappearing.

"You mean those rumors about him being a gangster."

"Most of these businessmen are. Probably all of them. Just like the politicians and the generals. They traded in Marxism for crony capitalism. They became what they thought they were driving out."

"Oldest story in the book," Levon said, wiping his bowl clean with a corner of the last pastry.

"You know way more than you're saying."

"You think I know something that you could sell on?"

"You know something. But you don't know enough to act on it."

"Maybe we could trade intel," Levon said.

"You know Le Duan? It's a street in District One. It ends in the east at a park. There's a statue of General Giap," she said as she scooted from the booth. She pulled on her raincoat.

"I can find it." He made to rise, and she patted the air to beckon him to remain seated.

"Meet me there at noon," she said. "I might have something for you, but you'll need to do something for me in return."

"Look, I could drive you to wherever—"

She cut him off, her nose wrinkling.

"You're not my type, cowboy."

He turned in his seat to respond to that, but she was already halfway to the open front of the store, raising the hood of her raincoat to step out into the storm.

9

Anchorage

BILL MARQUEZ WAS TIRED. He thought he might be coming down with something. Maybe it was just the long Alaska nights and the dreary Alaska days.

Bureau work was always a grind. Even more so than regular police work. FBI agents were more lawyer than cop. There were protocols and details and a kind of backward thinking to the whole federal process. It's more about building a case than finding a suspect. And the paperwork was hell. Most nights, Bill dreamed in triplicate.

But sometimes, if an agent ate all his vegetables and said his prayers, a break came his way. Not this time. The broccoli went down hard, and God was not picking up on his end. The Alaska trip was a wash for everyone but Lewis Dollinger, former deputy sheriff, Perry County.

They had Levon Cade dead bang for the homicide victims found on his property back in Alabama and the ones down in Idaho. He was in flight. So was his family. They'd all gone to ground. And Cade was a man who knew how to run and knew how to hide. The DoJ had all they needed to build the case. Now all they needed was the man.

And, frankly, the bureau had a shit record at finding folks who didn't want to be found. The Unibomber needed a relative to turn him in. Eric Rudolph made fools of them for years before a chance witness spotted him scrounging for food behind a Save-A-Lot. And it was a dog found that Brazilian midget in Pennsylvania a few months back. And not even a bureau dog.

The only lead to Cade was this Tranh character. Find him and they could get an idea of where Cade might be or might be heading. Though Bill doubted the little man would give anything up. The Asian gangs were tight. It was hard to work a wedge in, to offer any threats worse than those suffered by a rat who dared to turn on his masters.

And what had Cade done to make an outfit like that come for him? Most likely it all led back to the events in Maine when Cade first came on the radar. It had to do with the fortune in cash and the leads to the overseas accounts that Cade gave up a few years back to buy himself some peace with the government.

All that goodwill vanished when he killed those liquor men in Alabama and took off west. The bureau dug up a damned graveyard on the Cade farm near Colby. And now a fresh one in Idaho. Four bodies buried near a vintage Mustang hidden in a ravine on government land behind the ranch. Seemed like everywhere Cade called home turned into a killing ground.

Nothing had come of the facial recognition search other than Bill getting to spend phone time with Agent Elizabeth Ann Rigby and the promise that they'd do lunch when he got back to DC. She was single, thirty and her bureau portrait revealed she was every bit as cute as she sounded.

The promise of a lunch date was the best he could do. Tranh or Fong or Park or Ketukaeo, or whatever name he was traveling under currently, had not turned up anywhere on camera in either search area. He'd kept his word to Dollinger who'd be getting transferred as a guest of the federal government to a level one facility at Sierra Conservation Center just a few miles from Yosemite in California.

Having no more business in Anchorage and looking down into a deep dry hole, it was time to head back to DC for reassignment. He packed his bag and took a cab to Merrill Field. Bill had lucked out by being allowed to catch a government jet that was deadheading back to DC to pick up a bunch of congressmen for a junket. No hassling at Ted Stevens and cramming into a coach seat. He'd have the Gulfstream all to himself.

The cab dropped him off at the steel shack that served as a terminal building on the small city-owned field. He badged through security and hopped in the suicide seat of a golf cart to be taken out to the blue and white government jet spinning up for an early morning take-off.

Even with his shades on, Bill squinted against the glare off the snow heaps that rose in high banks down either side of the strip of tarmac. The morning was damp and cold, and the motion of the open cart created a wind with its passage that made Bill pull his coat tighter across his shoulders. The government plane sat at the far end of the field just past a sleek-looking Citation Bravo taking on luggage and passengers from an SUV pulled up alongside.

Bill studied the jet idly. It was a pretty number with a yellow tail and underbelly. The fuselage was marked with a Pran-Air logo in red cursive with a row of Asian characters below. Airport workers were loading luggage from the rear hatch of the Suburban into the open cargo hold in the belly.

Three men stood at the foot of the access ladder while a crew member checked their documents. Two tall men in down jackets with a much smaller man in a cashmere coat standing between them. The smaller man wore a fur cap that made him look like a miniature Cossack.

"Son of a bitch," Bill said to himself.

"Sumpin' wrong?" the cart driver asked.

"Stop the cart! Stop it now!" Bill shouted and was clambering onto the wet runway even before the cart had come to a full stop.

He was running across the open tarmac toward the Citation, watching the two larger men get into the SUV. They pulled away leaving the smaller man to climb the steps up to the hatch with the crewmember walking behind, a carry-on in his hand.

Bill had his gun out and ID folder up as he breathlessly arrived at the foot of the steps.

"Bin Liu Tranh," he panted. "FBI."

That night, back in DC, Bill Marquez ate all his vegetables and sent a special thank you to the Big Guy.

10

Gunny Leffertz said:

"You know what's more dangerous than a Trojan horse? A Trojan pussy."

District One To Chu Chi

HE MET her at noon the next day. She was waiting at the base of a stone plinth atop which sat a larger-than-life bust in brass of an elderly Asian man with a chest full of ribbons. The sun had made a rare appearance and she wore her raincoat tied about her waist by its sleeves. She wore cargo shorts and an outsized T-shirt printed with the image of a Japanese pop star. Under either hand, she balanced a pair of bicycles.

"I borrowed these, so we have to bring them back in one piece," Kate said as he loaded the bikes into the rear of the

Jeep. He had to leave the tailgate down in order to accommodate them.

"This was the favor you wanted?" he said as he secured the bikes in place with a pair of bungees. "To go bike riding with you?"

"You know how, right?" She gave him a look of appraisal. "You never forget how, right?"

"I told you I'd have something for you," she said once they were seated and he'd pulled out of the cul-de-sac. She reached into a canvas bag she had slung over her shoulder and produced a rolled magazine. It was a slightly dog-eared copy of *Singapore Business Review*.

"Is that the magazine you told me about?"

"It pays to know a few packrats." She waved the magazine at a row of food stalls that lined one side of the broad avenue they'd pulled onto. "I didn't get lunch. Your treat and I'll drive you where we're going."

They ate in the car as she took the wheel. They each had a *banh mi* and a bottled tea. He leafed through the magazine as Kate navigated the hectic flow of traffic. The trick, as he learned watching her drive, was to never slow down. She kept at an even speed, jinking when it was called for and merging when it was not. Somehow, despite the whine of motorbikes, a cacophony of horns and shouts of drivers, she brought them around each roundabout on the first go-round and soon they were up a ramp onto an open highway heading north and west away from the city's congestion.

Helpfully, the magazine was in English as well as Malay and simplified Chinese. He found the article, a lengthy feature on Hung Chi Bao with pictures that never once referred to him as Benny.

He appeared to be a fit man in his fifties at the time of the photos. He wore western suits in each picture but one in which he was shown teeing off at a golf course. His features were broad with a wide mouth. His hair was cut sheer at the sides and worn longer on top with a carefully maintained look of casual disregard that remained consistent from photo to photo. One profile picture seemed composed with the main focal point the Phillipe Patek watch on the wrist below the hand he had poised at his chin in quiet contemplation. In each photo, he wore aviator-style glasses with varying degrees of tint.

Skimming the article, Levon learned nothing of any real use. It was a puff piece of one business cliché following another. He wondered if Hung had paid for the article as a self-promotion tool. It spoke of how he'd turned KWI from a loss leader to a "powerful player" and of its "diversified revenue streams" that made it a "safe bet in the often-fractious corporate environment of Southeast Asia."

"A real load of horseshit, huh?" Kate said as she drove, eyes invisible behind a pair of mirrored Ray-Bans.

"He'd have more gray in his hair since then," Levon said, studying the largest photo that took up an entire page at the start of the article. Hung stood, hands in pockets and legs shoulder-width apart in the shade of a banyan tree. Beyond which a large white building with a red tile roof could be seen.

"And some work done." Kate nodded. "All those high rollers jet over to Switzerland or Korea for a tuck there or an implant here."

"What do I need to do to repay you for this?" He gestured with the rolled magazine.

"You think that's all I dug up?" She turned to him with a look of exaggerated offense.

He waited, watching the vapor rising from the tops of the trees that crowded the verge on either side of the highway.

"Hung has a condo he uses when he's doing business in the city," she said. "It's the top three floors of a high rise in the Tan Thuan Tay ward. A mansion in the sky, if I can believe my source."

"A local source?"

"No *way* I'm asking anyone local about Hung." She shook her head. "Girl, I went to school with works at NPR. She's done some reporting on the unholy alliance between legit business and the gangs here."

"Where does he live when he's not in Saigon?"

"Boy, you ask a *lot*."

"You said he stays at this condo when he's in the city. That means he's not always in the city."

"He's got a place outside Bao Loc. That's farther north. Like a country home. Cheryl said it used to be a French rubber plantation."

"Could be the place in this picture," Levon said, holding the magazine open.

"Could be. *Could* be *Tan Son Nhat*. That's a country club near the airport." She turned the wheel to join a right lane that turned into an off-ramp off the highway. All Levon could see ahead was trees.

"Where are we?" he asked.

"Chu Chi."

"This is where I repay your favor?"

"It won't kill you, Tom. All you have to do is ride bikes with me around an industrial park. You're my cover. An American tourist out on a jaunt with his Viet honey."

"And Chu Chi is a place a tourist would go?"

"Oh yeah. There's an old Viet Cong tunnel complex there. In fact, if you hadn't lied about being a Canadian the tourism ministry would have *made* you come see it. That is after they took you to the war museum to see pictures of all the imperialist war crimes and hear lectures about how shitty America is."

"It hasn't been shitty to you," Levon said. He could see the glint of long steel rooftops through the thinning foliage as the access road joined a two-lane on which a truck passed them.

"My parents worked their asses off to make it good for me and my sister and brother. I'm a Philly girl now. Born and raised. It's cheesesteaks and the Flyers for me."

"My uncle was here. Sixty-eight through seventy. Says it was a beautiful place run by some of the worst people in the world."

"You could say that about every place. I'll bet you could say that about sweet home Alabama."

"I've run into my share of sons of bitches."

"And you're looking for one now." She spared him a long look over her sunglasses as she pulled the Jeep onto a grassy shoulder.

"Not until he was looking for me," Levon said, meeting her gaze.

HIS SHIRT WAS PLASTERED to him before he'd biked a hundred yards. There was no wind, and the humidity hung over everything like an invisible fog. His boots were unsuited for biking, his soles slipping off the pedals as he tried to maintain purchase.

Kate rode ahead of him at an easy pace, weaving back and forth across the strip of asphalt to allow him time to keep up. The sky ahead appeared bruised. Rain was coming and the dark clouds were piled atop one another to form an impossibly high purple range.

The road was a two-lane with a run-off ditch on either side filled with pea-green water. It wound through an industrial park of near identical steel buildings in neutral colors. Signs on posts sported company logos in English and Viet. Some were shiny and new. Others were crusted with rust around the edges and discolored by the sun.

They had to veer to one side or another to allow the occasional truck to pass. Each truck gave Kate a blast of its horn as it passed to which she answered with an upraised finger. Riding behind, Levon could see that this evinced a laugh from each driver who nodded his way as they passed.

The rain came, as it always did, with an abruptness that took the breath away. Kate was a wobbling phantom before him and he saw her braking, dropping her feet to the ground to bring her bike to a stop. She hopped off, and he did the same to follow her over the top of a dyke across the teeming run-off ditch. They pushed their bikes at a run under the shelter of some tamarinds growing just off the road.

The rain struck the leaves above with a patter that rose and fell as each new sheet of water marched over them. He stripped off his sopping cotton shirt and crouched in his sodden T-shirt and khakis. She removed her raincoat from under a clamp atop her bike's rear fender and laid it on the ground to sit on.

"You're not going to do much industrial spying through this rain," he said, raising his voice to be heard over the din.

"That's what you think," she said and removed a plastic case from the canvas bag she'd carried in the bike's front basket. Inside was a pair of binoculars. Levon recognized the brand.

"ATN Binox," she said, holding them out to him after making some adjustments to the control pad set in the shell between the lens barrels.

He took a look and could clearly see the buildings across the roadway despite the dense haze of falling water. The image was high contrast and monochromatic, a heavily digitized version of reality that made details that would have been invisible to the naked eye stand out.

"Pretty cool, huh?" she said, taking them back. "I was counting on the rain. It gives us an excuse to linger."

"And what are we looking for?" He twisted his cotton shirt in his fists to wring it out.

"Lots of things," she said, the lenses to her eyes. "This place across the road makes chemical fertilizer. They have a contract with a major agri-business in the US. I don't see a lot of activity over there."

"And that tells you...?"

"That maybe they're having trouble sourcing the components they need. Maybe they won't meet their contract quota. There's a mad rush for phosphates all over Asia. Could be this company got shut out of their sources, outbid by China or India."

"Which means the American company won't have what it needs for the next growing season."

"You see how it works," she said, turning from her view to smile at him. "Everything connects. A butterfly effect all around the world. I can see into the future through these things. I can see higher costs for produce. Scarcities. I can make sure one of my clients places his money right in the commodities market or shorts the American company to make a shitpile."

"I think we were better off when all we had was a shit-pile," Levon said, resting his back against the bole of the nearest tree.

"Is that some kind of hillbilly wisdom?" She sat on her raincoat and turned to him.

"Just a simple truth. You had the land. Animals shit on the land. That helped you grow food on the land. The more animals, the more shit. The more shit, the more animals you could raise and feed."

"I take it you're one of those anti-globalists?" She raised an eyebrow at him.

"I've seen where it leads," he said. Seen it over the sights of a rifle, he didn't say.

"You know, here we are, under a tree, the rain coming

down." She set the binoculars down on the raincoat beside and leaned back on her hands. "And we're talking about shit."

"What would you rather talk about?" He looked past her at the shifting gloom beyond the cover of the tree limbs.

"Like, why you aren't coming on to me," she said, her head canted.

"Sounds like you're coming on to me," he said, turning to look at her.

"No, I'm not. I'm just wondering. You're not gay." She smirked. "Maybe you don't have a China girl fantasy. Or maybe you don't get close to *anyone*."

He didn't respond.

"What are you here for?" she said, her eyes suddenly hard. "I don't mean here, with me, today. What did you come to *Saigon* for? What is Benny Hung to you?"

"It's something I have to do," he said, his voice low. He had to repeat it when she told him she couldn't hear his reply.

"You said he was looking for you," she said, turning fully on the raincoat to face him. "What does he want from you?"

"Something I took that he believed was his."

"Money? A woman?"

"I think it's more a matter of pride with him."

"And you?" she asked, studying his eyes for the truth in his reply. "What's it a matter of for you?"

"My family," he said.

"Jesus," she breathed. "You're not *with* anyone. This is all *you*. This is all-*in* for you. Last man standing shit."

"A friend of mine says I'm looking for a samurai ending." Levon shrugged.

"It'd be a lot simpler if all you wanted to do was fuck me," Kate said, her crooked smile returning but failing to reach her eyes.

11

Gunny Leffertz said:
"You can't kill 'em if you can't find 'em."

Chim Công Tower

THE NEXT MORNING, Saigon was between rains. The sky was the color of slate, and the street was a steam bath. Levon walked from the Sofitel to a street nearby where he'd seen a row of electronics stores. From there, he caught a cab just as the sky opened up.

His driver's smile broadened when he heard English. The guy kept up a patter all the way across town to the Tan Thuan Tay section down along the river.

"Chim Cong is beautiful building. Much money," the driver said, turning from the wheel to make certain Levon was listening.

"It means *paon*. You know *paon*?" The driver splayed the fingers of one hand made a screeching sound.

"You mean peacock?" Levon said.

"Có! Yes! It is peacock!" the driver hooted with delight. "We call tower Chim Công Vàng. Is Golden Peacock."

Levon couldn't see anything golden about the dark edifice looming up through the murk as they approached. The driver pulled up under a broad portico where an attendant in a starched white Nehru jacket and pants with red piping opened the rear door. Levon dropped a Canadian twenty on the front seat of the cab. The driver's calls for "good fortune and the best of days to you, sir" were cut off when the attendant slammed the door shut. The cab sped away, disappearing into the veil of rain beyond the portico roof.

"Do you have business here or perhaps visiting an acquaintance?" the attendant asked in rote-learned English.

"I have an appointment to see a dentist," Levon said, a hand to his jaw.

"Most excellent," the attendant gestured for Levon to follow him through a bank of revolving doors and into the vault-ceilinged lobby of black marble streaked with red and tan. The attendant stood before a wall on which a building directory was mounted. There were business names and logos as well as doctor's practices that took up the bottom floors of the building above which were private residences, condos, and apartments. And above these, the multi-floored urban hideout of Benny Hung.

"It is here—here you—" The attendant hesitated to recall the words necessary to complete his next line.

"This is good. This is okay." Levon pressed some folded bills into his hand. The man bowed and smiled a fixed smile but did not leave.

Levon studied the directory. Rows of black engraved panels slid into brass frames. Each entry was in three languages. French, Viet, and Lao. He found the name he'd Googled and pointed to it.

The attendant nodded and gestured for Levon to follow as they walked to a corridor at the back of the lobby lined either side with elevators. A car came and a small group of mostly men made for it. They were all Asians and dressed either in business suits or sports jackets without ties. Most had umbrellas under their arms. Levon also noted a pair of armed security guards in short-sleeved uniform shirts and black ball caps. They looked to be former military. Another wad of cash and the attendant left Levon to board on his own.

Another guy in a white uniform operated the elevator and understood zero English. Levon held up fingers for the seventh floor. This caused a whispered exchange among the other passengers. Someone stifled a snicker.

The doors opened at seven and Levon stepped out with a pair of guys in business suits. He made a show of studying the floor directory until the pair were out of sight around a turn in the hall.

The elevators having operators was going to be a complication. He wouldn't be free to roam the building that way. He walked along the hallway until he came to an intersection. A woman carrying a file box passed him without looking as he pretended to read the business names on the plaques set by each door. He came to a stairwell entrance and pushed the door open.

It was an auto-lock door that would not allow return access. He'd come prepared for this and peeled a strip of tape from a roll he'd bought that morning. He patted it securely over the bolt opening, making sure no tape would be visible to anyone walking by along the hall. He tested the firmness of the grip and was satisfied it was firm.

There were no cameras in evidence. The stairwell was a featureless tower of poured concrete slabs. This was bare-bones construction. Most of the budget for this tower went to exterior details to make the building showy.

The stairwell wasn't air-conditioned and felt like a sauna. What ventilation there was came from narrow slits in the outer walls. He could hear the rain spattering against the face of the building. The dry scent of limestone hung in the air. Rounded steel railings lined each stretch of stairs. He climbed upward, the scrape of his feet on the cement steps echoing upward.

He reached the fourteenth floor, soaked through. The stairwell ended here, the top landing walled on three sides by louvered steel slats. A fire door marked with a large "14" in plastic letters was set in a recess. He gave the panic bar a gentle press and found it was locked. There was a mortice lock system meant to deny entry to floors from the stairwell. The only unsecured door would be down on the ground floor or maybe the basement parking garage. He saw a metal box mounted atop the door frame. That was the power source for the lock and would connect to a central system to provide security with a way of unlocking certain floors in case of an emergency. He could probably defeat the lock that way, but it would leave a trace. He didn't want his presence in the building noticed.

Hung's "mansion in the sky" was six floors above and probably only accessible by a separate, private stairwell and private elevator. He could get this door open and gain access to the upper part of the building. But it would require some noise.

Levon removed the light jacket he was wearing and folded it to make a pad for him to sit on. He rested against the hard concrete wall to wait for the businesses below to close for the day and the building to empty.

———

THE FEEBLE LIGHT cast through the slits in the outer walls turned violet and then faded away entirely turning the throat of the stairwell dark as ink. Only his occasional movements caused the motion sensor light above the door to turn on. The stairwell cooled a bit as night came on turning the humidity to a clinging damp.

He stripped off his shirt and T-shirt and did fifty push-ups followed by some stretches. His phone told him it was eight in the evening. He ate two candy bars, chocolate-covered peanuts for sugar, and a bag of crisps for salt. He sipped at a 12-ounce water he'd brought along in his jacket pocket. When finished, he placed the candy and crisp wrappers inside the bottle and crushed it flat before returning it to his jacket pocket.

The stairwell backed up against one bank of elevator shafts. He could hear the cars moving up and down through the wall. The traffic grew less and less. By midnight he started counting off the intervals of elevator motion. When they reached thirty minutes apart, he pressed an ear to the cool steel of the door and listened. It was eighteen minutes past one.

Levon put on his T-shirt and reversed his jacket to expose a black lining. He pulled on a pair of black stretch-fabric gloves. He waited until he heard the elevator move once more. Almost exactly a half hour had passed when he heard the grind of the elevator motors through the concrete and the rush of a car descending. When the sound of its passage had drawn down to silence, he braced both hands against the panic bar.

Brute force worked when nothing else would. His boots set on the floor, he bunched his shoulders to thrust hard on the panic bar. The pad under his hands gave a bit. Maintaining pressure, he drove his right shoulder hard against the surface of the door. The lock disengaged with a pop and the door sprung open.

He stood, one foot on the carpet of a dark hallway, and listened. No alarm sounded. Wedging the door open with a boot, he applied a fresh strip of tape over the bolt opening and eased the door closed.

The dim corridor felt frigid after the oven confines of the stairwell. He moved at a fast walk along the hall and was surprised when ceiling lights blinked on as he passed. He stopped his progress and waited. The lights went off after thirty seconds. He moved in a circuit about the fourteenth floor looking for the entrance to the stairwell that would lead him to the upper levels.

The only exit he could find was a steel door set in a recess. Mounted on one wall to the right of the frame was a keypad with a card sensor. He crouched now, studying the pad. Force would not do here. This door served high-paying tenants and would absolutely be wired to a central security station somewhere in the building.

He rose and moved toward a niche in which a glass door was set back between two floor-to-ceiling panes with faux palms in decorative clay pots to either side. The door had names listed on it beneath a company logo featuring a tiger.

Levon waited, unmoving, and the lights in the hallway went dark once again. The floor was silent but for the hum of the ventilation and the peculiar ambiance of empty rooms. From somewhere on the floor, he heard the single chime of an elevator arriving. It was the thirty-minute mark, the guards making their rounds like clockwork.

He pressed himself to the wall of the niche and waited. The hallway grew brighter and brighter again as the guard approached, setting off the motion sensors. Levon drew down into a crouch, eyes on the carpet. The lights in the hallway beyond his niche flickered to life. A shadow fell across the far wall.

He let the man pass, remaining still until something, some sensory stimuli, made the man start to turn.

The man had a hand around the grip of his sidearm as Levon launched to snake an arm about his throat. It was an uneasy one-arm hold as Levon needed a free hand to clap around the guard's gun hand. His hand easily engulfed the smaller man's grip, preventing the guard from drawing, crushing fingers against the grip to keep them from the trigger.

As he drew the man, feet kicking, from the floor, Levon bent back the guard's wrist, hearing the joint pop. The guard's fingers went nerveless, his hold going limp as the feeling left his hand. Levon shook the gun free to fall to the carpet then quickly slipped the radio from its belt hook and dropped it to the floor.

Now able to use both hands, he secured the lock about the man's throat. The guard kicked at his shins and clawed his arms. Levon maintained the chokehold, cutting off the blood flow of the jugular and carotid.

Like a puppet whose strings have been cut, the man relaxed as though boneless to dangle in Levon's hold. Levon kept the pressure to a count of sixty. When there was no further movement, he eased the guard to the floor. He dropped the gun and radio on the man's belly and dragged him back to the stairwell door which he propped open with one boot to deposit the man on the landing there. He then crouched and unclipped a lanyard from the man's shirt front. Attached to this was a key entry card with a QR symbol under lamination. He took the radio and gun, a Russian-made Makarov, and tucked them into the waistband at the back of his khakis.

Levon made his way back to the security door that led to the upper stairwell. He brushed the screen with the key card and heard a click. He gave the door a tentative push to take a turkey peek inside. It was the bottom landing of an empty stairwell only air-conditioned and finished with two-tone painted walls and indirect lighting. The steps had rubber no-slip pads on them.

He made his way up the stairs moving two at a time. He was on the clock now. He had, by his rough count, less than twenty minutes before the security center would be wondering where their man was.

The doors above re-started the floor count at fifteen running to twenty before he reached a door marked with a large numeral one. This would indicate the first floor of the Hung penthouse. He approached cautiously, his back to the wall as he surveyed the area around the door. Once again, he was surprised to find no cameras in evidence. It was either hubris, neglect, or the simple fact that the elite class had little to fear from petty criminals in the oligarchic state that Vietnam had become.

Gun in hand, he swiped the entry card over the screen. Nothing happened. He swiped it again.

The code for this door was different than those below. The door was also unlike the others, as there was no panic bar or lever. The door was just a featureless metal slab. There weren't any hinges visible. No way to hack it. No way to force it in.

And it was a certainty that, despite not taking any electronic precautions, Hung would have bodyguards present if he was in residence. Even if Levon could force the door, he'd have guns on him before he ever gained access.

He moved away from the door and climbed up to the next level. The two floors above had doors of the same kind. He continued on up two long flights into the mechanical levels at the top of the building. These walls were not painted, and the lighting was bare bulbs in ceiling fixtures. Rain hammered down on the ribbed steel roof that capped the stairwell.

An unsecured door gave him access to the roof. He opened the door and was immediately soaked in a gale-force torrent. Moving to shelter between rows of air conditioning cooling towers, Levon crossed the roof to the foot of a raised platform.

A helicopter sat atop the pad there. A yellow Leonardo with black trim was tied down under a tarp, its rotors securely lashed in place. Levon climbed the steps toward it and raised a flap of the tarp to duck under.

Out of the rain now, he opened the co-pilot hatch. A corrugated rubber mat, cut around the floor controls, covered the floor of the cockpit. He peeled back a corner of the mat. From a pocket of his khakis he took a GPS smart tracker, a baby blue plastic triangle no bigger than the end of his thumb. He placed it on the floor and pressed the floor mat back in place over it.

He climbed inside to reach between the pilot and co-pilot's seat and open a console set between two upholstered passenger seats. He dropped a second tracker inside and pushed a hand in to make sure it was well down under the contents. A third tracker he simply tossed to the rear of the passenger cabin where it dropped behind a bench seat bolted to the rear wall.

Back inside the stairwell, he retraced his steps down to the fourteenth floor and the main stairwell. Here, he removed the tape from the door bolt. He resecured the gun and radio onto the guard's belt. He looped the keycard lanyard about his neck before lifting the man from the floor into a fireman's carry.

He carried the body over his shoulder and down two flights. There he poised himself atop a flight before bending double to fling the lifeless form down the steps. The guard landed, arms akimbo, legs crossed and head at an ugly angle, at the foot of the steps. Levon stepped over him to descend down to the seventh floor where he removed the tape from that door before exiting into the corridor.

He found a men's room where he stripped to his boxers

to dry himself as best he could with handfuls of paper towels. He leaned over a tap at a row of sinks and drank his fill. He checked his phone. The three trackers were sending.

All that remained was the waiting.

Taking up residence inside a stall, Levon hung his jacket, shirt, and khakis from the hook inside the door. Here he would bide his time until morning when he could mix with the daytime visitors and exit the building unnoticed.

Gunny Leffertz said:

"You got to know when to get out and then get your ass OUT."

Flight

LEVON CABBED BACK to the Sofitel for a shower followed by a room service breakfast. While eating, he checked his phone. The trackers were five by five. The helo was still atop Peacock Tower. A heavy rain was still falling so it was likely to stay there. There was little for him to do but wait.

It was time to visit DannCo again, if only for the sake of appearances. The same pair of receptionists greeted him and asked who he wished to see. Levon said he only wanted access to any vacant workstation. He flashed the ID badge that Carl Winninger had given him on his last visit. One of the receptionists showed him back into the area of cubicles he'd seen before and handed him over to an office manager who took him to a cubicle.

The cubicle's desk was bare but for a keyboard and monitor and a plastic pen cup. Half the space inside was taken up with a double stack of cardboard file boxes.

He began a Google Map and property search of the Bao Loc area for the possible location of Hung's rural home. There were easily two dozen holdings that might be candidates. Maybe even more seized back in the bad old days following the American pull-out. There was no way to learn how many were former French plantations without further digging.

His initial survey of the area reminded him of home. The small city of Bao Loc sat at a crossroads at the foot of a long valley lined either side by green mountains covered in triple canopy forest. The larger estates were all situated up on what would have been called hollers back in Alabama. A few had visible access roads that led to tile-roofed mansions set on broad cleared areas of either pasture or paddies. Other roads branched off the main highway to vanish under the cover. The homes or compounds that lay at the end of those winding driveways were invisible to Google's satellite surveys.

Carl Winninger stepped into the cubicle to lean over him close enough to fill Levon's nose with the man's aftershave.

"Someone came around asking about you," Winninger said. He made his displeasure known with each syllable.

Levon turned to him.

"They didn't show badges," Winninger went on. "They didn't have to. But judging from the quality of their suits, I'd say they were state security."

"How long ago?"

"Yesterday afternoon."

It wasn't about last night.

"I shined them on with some bullshit about you meeting with local vendors," Winninger said, stepping aside to allow Levon to rise. "I don't need this."

"I won't be back," Levon pocketed his phone.

Winninger wasn't done. He followed Levon out into the lobby, making a show of it.

"Do you know what I have to do to grease the fucking pirates who run this country? I paid you. I gave you cover. You have my money. Your cover's blown."

Levon didn't respond as he walked for the exit doors. He noted that the receptionists were no longer smiling. Their eyes studied Winninger, taking in every word of the harangue that continued until Levon was out in the rain once more.

He drove the Jeep from the lot and wound his way back toward the central districts via a route that wound through residential areas and finally a service road that ran along rail tracks. No one was tailing him. They probably didn't have to. The Jeep would have a tracker or two hidden somewhere inside.

For now, whoever was interested in him was just curious. They were punching the clock by following around newly arrived foreigners. Only his ID, good as it was, wouldn't stand up to the kind of questions a state security agency would ask. If they weren't already onto Thomas Creighton of Montreal being a total fiction, then they would be as soon as they pulled a few more threads.

The rain died away as he drove between apartment blocks and down a road that ended at a "T" intersection. There was a park there with a few scabby kapok trees fringing a soccer pitch. Taking advantage of a break in the downpour, a crowd of kids were out kicking a ball around. They were coated in mud as the field had become a swampy mire. A bunch of other kids sat along a bench smoking counterfeit Marlboros and calling out to the players.

Levon pulled the Jeep to a stop along a curtain wall that separated the park from the roadway. One of the kids on the bench turned his way as he killed the engine. Two more watched as he stepped out of the Jeep and dangled the key fob for them to see.

He pitched the fob over the wall onto the grass and turned away to cross the road through a stream of scooters and jitneys. He walked south a ways in the direction of the Sofitel. He'd gone a few blocks when he heard a horn toodle. His Jeep zipped by him down the rain-wet street, the kids from the bench crowded inside calling and laughing.

Another few blocks brought him to a broad boulevard where he hailed a pedicab just as the rains returned.

———

THE LOBBY of the Sofitel was thronged with a lunchtime crowd. He'd only be there long enough to change from his sodden clothes into something dry.

Levon cut between groups chatting or standing by piles of luggage to reach the elevators. He stopped when he saw Kate Nhan rise from a sofa in a waiting area. She wore her red raincoat and closed a book that was in her lap as she rose.

"I have something for you," she said as she stepped in his path, holding the book before her.

"Let's have lunch. On me." He took her arm and turned her toward the doors.

She trotted to keep up, only pulling her arm away when they'd stepped out under the portico.

"What's going on?" she said, brows knitted.

"You can't stay here," he said and gestured toward a cab

sitting along a curb in the rain beyond the shelter of the portico.

"At the Sofitel?" she asked.

"In Vietnam." He bustled her into the rear of the cab.

THEIR CONVERSATION DID NOT RESUME until they were at a rear booth in a noisy bar, a laughable attempt to recreate an English pub called The Pork and Cow.

"What are you talking about?" she asked after their drink orders were taken.

"You have to get out of this country. Today. Right now. Go to Thailand or Australia. Whatever the earliest flight is." He was feigning interest in the menu which featured "Real Shepherd's Pie."

"Just like that?" She lowered her voice to a whisper that did nothing to hide her irritation. "Are you in some kind of trouble? Am *I* in trouble?"

"There'll be questions. You don't want to be around to answer them." He dug in a pocket and came up with a fat wad of bills. Mixed Canadian dollars and Viet dong.

"What's this?" She looked at the bills he set before her.

"It's enough to get you out of here."

"Do I get to pack?"

"No. You leave from here. Pick up some luggage and some clothes on the way. You can't pay cash *and* travel without baggage."

"What if I had a cat?"

"Do you have a cat?"

"No. But what if I *did*?"

He reached over the table and took her hand in his. She froze, his touch startling her.

"This might be nothing," he said, pressing her fingers together. "Only I can't ask you to take that chance. I don't know when they landed on me, but you and I spent a couple of days together. We've been seen together."

"Are you doing this because you're worried about me or because you don't trust me?"

"My name is Levon Cade. I'm from Haley County, Alabama. I'm here to kill Benny Hung."

"Does that mean you trust me?"

"It gives you something to bargain with in case they stop you. You tell them who I am and why I'm here."

Eyes hard on his, she pulled her hand from his grip. He snatched at her sleeve as she scooted her chair back and got to her feet. She shouldered through the line of customers until she was framed in the weak light of the open front door.

She left the roll of cash in a puddle on the tabletop.

Gunny Leffertz said:

"*Strike and move. Strike and move. Never be where they think you are.*"

The Road To Bao Loc

"WHICH YOU WANT?" the vendor said, gesturing at a row of colorful boxes crammed into shelves behind his counter. "All good. All best kind. Which you want?"

"The blue box." Levon had to raise his voice to be heard over the noise of competing voices and music in the crowded market. He pointed at the box he wanted and held up two fingers.

"Good ones. Fun for kids." The vendor got down two boxes roughly six inches square. They were VIN-PRO 600 mini drones. Knockoffs for a million *dong* each. About forty bucks. He added a pair of re-charge batteries and three Nokia phones and four Mobifone re-up cards for them. It all came to just under two hundred bucks. The vendor asked for his passport. Levon peeled off a half million VND to keep the sale private.

At a second stall, he bought a pair of 30X binoculars and a digital camera, a Canon knockoff, with a telephoto lens along with batteries and the other accessories he'd need.

He stuffed the new purchases into his carry-on and melted into the mob of tourists shuffling along the aisles of the Ben Thanh Market, a barn of a place with over a thousand market stalls. Outside, he snagged a pedicab and asked for the nearest bus station. Once there, he paid cash for a round-trip seat on a bus leaving north for Da Lat the next morning. He paid cash and used a fallback passport for a Dennis Vogel from Wilmington, Delaware, to book the seat. The bus was scheduled to make a stop in Bao Loc just after one in the afternoon.

From there, he got on one of the red city buses that snaked around the city carrying locals and tourists. He rode until he saw a sign for an internet kiosk. As it grew darker outside, the steel gray sky turning violet, he paid for a station inside the kiosk to boot up the new phones and charge his battery packs.

It was a full night by the time he stepped out onto the street again into a teeming rain. He boarded another bus and looked out onto the dark streets seen through the pall of water. The bus made its pokey way along a broad boulevard crossing dim streets until it reached the center of the city once more. Here, wide avenues branched away looking like neon-limned canyons.

Levon stepped off the bus to wade into the foot traffic moving in a steady current along the rows of clubs, bars, shops, and booths that lined the street. The rain hissed and spat off the electric signage that hung high overhead and ran along the marquees of the larger places.

Rather than book a room, Levon moved through the night like just another foreign lookie-loo. It was an all-night scene and would provide him with a refuge until the bus left the following morning. He took up a stool at bars near others traveling together so, to the casual witness, he looked to be a member of their party. He struck up a few conversations and paid for a few rounds. Once with a large group of Pakistanis here for a bachelor party. Another time he spent an hour with some Germans celebrating their last night in country.

In the hours before dawn, he broke away from the crowds, leaving the garish lights behind to walk along one of the narrow alleys that wound away from the strip. Levon weaved, feigning a drunk, down a sidewalk lined with shuttered shops and apartment entrances. A steady flow of water raced along the gutters topped with paper wrappers and plastic cups. Wherever the alley intersected with another street a temporary lake formed as the drains were overwhelmed by the downpour.

Two or three turns brought him to a street barely wide enough for a car to pass between the high curbing on either side. Asphalt had worn away in spots to show the cobblestone road surface beneath. Old colonial-style buildings rose up to a strip of pinkish sky. Rain made a tattoo on the slats of louvered shutters and gurgled down clay spouts to gush in torrents into the street. It might have been an older section of Paris on a stormy night.

Levon stumbled as he crossed one of these rushing streams. He leaned against a wall for support, bending double as if dizzy. He stayed there, watching from under his brows as two figures separated from the shadows cast by an awning over a building entrance.

Two men approached him, separating to come at him

from either side, one in the street, the other on the walk. They wore hoodies decorated with soccer team colors. Levon remained bent double, hunching his shoulders as though preparing to vomit.

The one on the walk thrust a hand down along his side. Metal gleamed in his hand. A butterfly knife. The one on the street moved to come around behind.

Levon came out of his crouch to snatch the wrist of the knife man in his grip. It was like holding the arm of a child. Turning, he pulled the knife man toward him. The knife man took the blow from an escrima stick meant for Levon. He called out, voice high. Perhaps it was the name of his partner. Levon bent the knife wrist until he felt a wet crunch before shoving the knife man into the stick man. He caught the folding knife as it fell.

The knifeman was on his knees in the street, holding his broken wrist. The stick man recovered and lunged for Levon who batted the stick aside. Levon drove the double-edged dagger blade into the muscle at the top of the stick man's thigh. He followed up with a drive to the man's face with the heel of his hand. He felt something pop through his palm. The stick man collapsed in a heap over the curb.

Levon turned his attention to the knifeman who was trying to rise while holding his injured arm supported by his other hand. Levon took him by the front of his hoodie and dragged him upright. After a quick pat-down, he pulled aside the man's hoodie to reveal the acne-scarred face of a kid who couldn't be more than sixteen. Levon shoved him against a wall.

"You know English? American?"

The kid shook his head.

"*Comprenez-vous le français?*"

The kid shrugged, eyes on Levon.

"*Je veux acheter une arme à feu. Tu ne sais pas où je peux acheter un pistolet?*"

The kid squinted at him, lips curling in bewilderment.

He'd looked up the phrase he'd need on a translation site. He didn't have time to practice his pronunciation. French was not a strong suit.

"*Une arme. Une pistolet.*" Levon made his hand into a gun, poking the index finger into the kid's face. "I want to buy. Dollars," he said in English.

The kid nodded now. Gesturing with his head back the way Levon had come.

They left the stick man lying unconscious in the gutter, rainwater eddying around him.

THE KID KNEW a guy who knew a guy.

It was early morning, weak sunlight turning shadows to a hazy gloom in the narrow streets. Far from the beaten track of the tourists, local stalls and shops were opening up. One of these was a fish market. The kid, nursing his arm and talking fast, spoke to a man in a rubber apron who was unloading crates of carp from the back of a rusted and sagging Hilux pickup. The guy narrowed his eyes at Levon through a swirl of smoke from the butt of the cigarette clamped between his lips. He shooed the kid with the broken wrist away and gestured for Levon to follow him into his shop.

Women stood working at wooden tables, gutting fish with expert ease. An elderly man shoveled ice into plastic tubs from the mouth of a wheezing ice machine. The guy in the rubber apron parted the plastic strips of a divider curtain and waved Levon inside.

The guy rubbed his fingers together in the universal sign language of "where's your money?" Levon held up a thick roll of ten thousand *dong* notes. It added up to ten million VND. This was no place to be flashing his full wad. The guy undid the rubber band and counted it out on the top of a steel desk. Satisfied, he unlocked a standing cabinet and laid his wares on the desktop.

The selection was poor. A Czech made Makarov with most of the factory blueing worn off. Levon opened the action and held it to light to see that the barrel was pitted. There was a German Luger from God knew where. It was in worse condition than the Czech gun. It rattled when he shook it.

The best of the lot was a French MAB pistol chambered in nine-millimeter. The grips were long gone, replaced with layers of friction tape. But the action worked smooth, the hammer and firing pin intact and the interior of the barrel was still shiny.

Levon held up the empty magazine. The fish man rubbed his fingers together with a shrug. Two million more *dong* bought a box of cartridges and a spare magazine.

He wrapped the pistol, ammo, and magazine in some newspapers he took from a stack in the fish cutting room and left the shop. Moving at a trot, he found his way from the maze to a main avenue where he hailed a cab.

The bus was loading when he got to the station. He showed the driver his ticket and Dennis Vogel passport and boarded.

The bus was packed with gabbling tourists stowing carry-ons and settling into seats. The claustrophobic interior featured one row of double seats across from an aisle of single seats. Stacked atop these was another tier of seats. Each was capable of reclining to allow the occupant to lie nearly supine as in an easy chair. A petite Dutch woman gratefully traded her upper berth seat for Levon's lower.

He climbed up into the seat in the back row to find a boy of about eleven in the window seat fully engrossed in a Dutch-language Harry Potter paperback. The petite woman's son, he assumed. The boy barely acknowledged his seatmate's presence.

Levon worked a lever which dropped his seat back and raised a leg support. Even as tall as was, he managed to stretch full out and was soon fast asleep.

He did not awake until he felt the bus jerking to a halt and the driver calling out their first stop in Bao Loc.

14

Philadelphia

THE WHOLE FAMILY was there to meet her at baggage claim. Kate Nhan was exhausted after a day and half of travel with layovers in Australia and San Diego. All she wanted to do was go home to her old room and sleep for a week.

All her sisters, brothers, nephews, and nieces wanted was for her to tell them what the old country was like. All her mother wanted to do was feed her. All her father wanted to do was get back to the main store in Abington.

Mom won out. She always did. Their caravan of two cars stopped at a Chinese buffet (owned by Viets like they all were) in Elkins Park.

Over noodles, rice, spring rolls, and raspberry tea, Kate told them everything she'd seen leaving out the White guy and the reasons for her sudden departure. She told them they would not recognize Saigon. She told them about the shops and hotels and skyscrapers. She told them it smelled like New Jersey there.

It was night by the time they pulled into the driveway at her parents' house and all piled out. Her father and brother took her luggage. Her mother ran a bath for her. She lay back in the steaming tub with a damp washcloth over her face and felt the kinks of the long plane rides melt away.

A timid tapping at the door woke her from a twilight state. It was her grandmother, her mother's mother.

"Yes, Bá?" Kate asked as the stooped old lady took a seat on the toilet lid.

"You are sad, rúa nhó," her grandmother stated. Little turtle. A name from her childhood. A name her grandmother had given her from all the times the old woman had taken her to her swimming lessons at the Y.

"Just tired, Bá."

"You were not to come home until summer."

"A change in plans."

The old woman nodded sagely.

"I'll be home for a while."

"What will you do?"

"Maybe look for a new job. I might go back to school for a few courses."

"Will you return to Đông Dương?" A very old name for Vietnam.

"I can't, Bá," Kate said and was surprised to find her eyes welling with tears.

"It is best, rúa nhó," her grandmother said, rising. "If, as you say, our country is no more."

15

Gunny Leffertz said:

"As some old jarhead said, 'To catch us, you have to be fast. To find us, you have to be smart. To beat us, you have to be kidding.'"

The Hunt

HIS NEW CAMERA slung around his neck and bag over his shoulder, Levon moved away from the passengers stepping off the bus to stretch their legs. Some wandered into the station to use the restrooms or dump coins into the rows of vending machines. Others used the opportunity for a smoke. The driver called out repeated warnings in four languages that this was a thirty-minute break only.

Levon followed the half dozen or so passengers walking with luggage wheeled behind them for a rank of pedicabs.

He walked past the cabs, ignoring the gaggle of guys waving brochures and hawking guided tours of the town.

He hiked west along a four-lane street with a row of tea trees planted in a long row on the median strip. Playing tourist, he stopped and snapped a few pictures. It was midday and the heat and humidity had driven most of the locals into the shade. The sun was visible at the top of a dome of sky ringed by dark clouds.

Bao Loc sat at the center of a broad bowl of land. All around the town rose green heights, the lower slopes terraced to grow coffee and the variety of tea the place was famous for. The heights were like battlements holding back the clouds to create a temporary relief from the rains. Levon could see a gray haze marching down from the ridge tops where rain was falling. The eye would close soon and the town would be engulfed.

He skirted around traffic circles and pocket parks and walked along the low wall of a cemetery crowded with rows of concrete tombs and tiny shrines stained with black mold. He came to a marketplace packed with stalls, some in the open and others under the cover of faded awnings.

One of the merchants was selling army surplus. War souvenirs for the tourists. There were packs and webbing and piles of uniforms and helmets of US and NVA image. A glass case of medals and unit patches for ARVN, Marine and Army regiments. Levon suspected most of these were counterfeit. He sorted through a pile of NVA rucksacks until he found one with straps the least worn and the buckles free of rust. It featured a patch sewn across the main flap, a yellow star against red and blue bars. He also bought a tattered Boonie hat and poncho with hood in olive drab.

His last purchase was a K-Bar knife in a battered steel sheath. He drew the long, pointed blade of the dagger and was pleased to see the dark steel still had an oily sheen. The leather handle had long ago rotted away but he could easily replace it with tape. It felt familiar in his hand, the weight of it, the balance. It was a weapon he'd come to regard as an extension of himself since his days on Parris Island and at SERE. It was a Marine weapon.

He used the rucksack like a shopping bag, stowing bottled water and pre-packaged food in its pouches. He also bought a pair of dark green pullovers and a bag of white socks after a bit of a search for his size with the help of a merchant and his pair of giggling children.

The cleanest looking of the food stalls offered barbecued pork, greens, and glass noodles for under three bucks. Two more for two bottles of iced Tiger beer. He ate and drank his fill and followed along with the general flow of foreign tourists, mostly couples in their twenties. College students on break, he guessed. He did the sightseeing thing before following a winding road that led down toward a lake. Here he booked a room in a hostel using his Dennis Vogel ID.

The room featured a bunk bed with drawers underneath with just enough room left over for a small writing desk and straight-back wicker chair.

The steady drizzle that had blotted out the sun in the afternoon turned to a deluge as the monsoon broached the surrounding hills to turn the sky a burnished bronze.

The impact of water on the roof of the hostel turned to a steady roar as Levon stripped off his clothes and hung them to dry on pegs. The new phones were unpacked and plugged into the reserve batteries to bring them to full charge. He sat naked on the bed and read through the manual for the drones. He organized his pack, arranging the items inside for the best distribution of weight and ease of access for items he might have the most frequent need of.

Once the pack was secured, he stripped the MAB and cleaned each piece with an oiled rag before reassembling it and wrapping it in the same rag.

The phones topped off, he plugged in the drones and set them aside to charge.

He lay back on the bunk to listen to the steady beat of rain and wait for the dark.

⊏⊐

THE RAIN WAS STILL COMING down in a steady gush when he slipped out to move down the narrow hall that ran between the rooms. He had the poncho draped over him to cover the pack on his back. Underneath the poncho, he wore both pullovers under his coat. There was a faint flickering light from under one of the doors. Someone watching something on a laptop or tablet. The rest of the rooms were dark. Outside, water streamed off the roof and ran down the floor of the alley that led to the street where it pooled around a drain.

The street was dark and free of motor or foot traffic. Levon pulled up the hood of the poncho and took off at a steady walk on a generally westerly course. Where the street divided to go around a park, he kept straight to cut through the trees to the other side. The street was stacked on either side with homes and apartments. The lots became broader, the homes larger and more spread out. Asphalt gave way to an unpaved roadway that led between orchards of tea trees set in neat rows. There was a gentle incline building before the road ended at a steel tractor barn.

Levon moved past the barn through rows of trees. The rain hissed down through the leaves turning the ground under his feet to clinging mud. He kept his path to places where water came down the hillside in streams. Any sign of his passage would be washed away by morning.

The way ahead was steeper now as the trail climbed toward the ridge line invisible now through the thick foliage that grew beyond the edges of the tea farms.

He could feel the cool night air through the poncho and his multiple layers of clothing. This part of the country, the central highlands, was cooler at night than down around Saigon. The rain added to the chill.

Three hours of steady upward climbing brought him to a ledge that was rimmed by a rocky shelf covered in moss. He rested atop the brow of rock, winded from the hump up the thirty-degree angle of the slope. Through the constant white noise of the drops falling through the leafy canopy above he could hear a rumble like thunder. It was the boom of one of the waterfalls that ran into the bowl of Bao Loc. The water was running at capacity now, fed by swollen streams running down the crown of the hill.

Levon crouched, the poncho forming a tent over him. His exertions caused him to sweat despite the cooler air. He drank from a water bottle and munched on a protein bar he'd picked up at the market. It had a red bean base and was spicy rather than sweet.

He couldn't help but think of Fern. His uncle was here, a green Marine arriving just two weeks before the Tet Offensive in '68. Maybe Fern humped these same hills hauling his "pig," the M-60 he'd spoken of like a friend whenever he shared memories of those days. And he only ever shared them Levon, opening up only to someone who'd understand.

Fern would stay for three tours, re-enlisting for the last one. It wasn't until a year or so back that he told Levon why he re-upped. It was a deal he cut so that Levon's father would not have to see combat. Both Cade boys had enlisted in the corps, Fern being the oldest, went first.

Once he saw battle himself, Fern wanted to spare his little brother the hell of it. Experienced men, anyone who had survived their first tour, were prized over cherry troops. The men who'd learned the lessons that would allow them to survive here were encouraged to stay on. Levon's uncle agreed to stay in a combat unit so long as his brother was assigned only to peaceful postings. So, Levon's father spent his enlistment in California and then two years stationed on Okinawa, the closest he'd ever get to Vietnam.

"I did it for our mama mostly," Fern told Levon. "Your father was always her favorite of all of us. If he died, she'd have died with him. I never wanted to see that."

"Did he ever know?" Levon said.

"That I was why he didn't end up in the shit? He thought it was his own luck. Your Grandma thought it was her prayers. They must have all been for your dad 'cause I never got *my* ass Jesus'ed out of there."

"Why didn't you tell him?"

"You remember your dad well enough to know he didn't like owing favors. Especially ones he couldn't ever repay. There was enough friction between us. I wasn't about to go adding to it."

Levon looked out over the shifting gloom and thought on what it took to volunteer to come back here for two more tours. Long tours. The Army tour of duty was one year in-country. Uncle Sam's Misguided Children had to go that one better. Thirteen months.

Now here Levon was, a generation later, stomping through the bad bush.

Repaying his daddy's debt.

THE NEXT MORNING brought a dense fog that rose out of the valley in a steamy mist. Levon had found shelter under the cover of a heaped mound of fallen timber. It protected him from the downpour and allowed him to build a small fire to partly dry off. He banked the blaze to hide its glow. The smoke rose to be dissipated by the rain.

The monsoon had abated leaving behind a cloying haze

as thick as smoke and white as cotton. The world around Levon's improvised refuge was reduced to only what he could see at a distance of ten feet. A milky glow was building from the east as the sun crested the highlands. The fog would burn away within the hour.

Levon laced up his boots over a fresh pair of socks and shouldered his backpack for a brisk climb toward the summit of the slope invisible somewhere in the cloud above him. When he reached a quarter-acre clearing just shy of the ridgeback, he took one of the drones from the pack and attached a burner phone to its undercarriage after activating the tracker app and camera.

The drone sputtered to life with a high whining sound. He sent it aloft where it vanished in the swirling cover of mist that clung to the treetops. The view on the control screen was a skein of shifting white pixels only coming into focus once the little drone was above the fog bank and into the pink-hued morning sky.

He guided the drone to fifteen hundred feet above his location. It would be invisible to anyone on the ground. At that height, the whir of the four tiny propellers could not be heard.

The drone zoomed away to the north where he brought it to a stop where the green-topped hills began. Recalling what he read in the manual, he set the drone on a circular course that would roughly describe the ring of peaks that encircled the Bao Loc area. His phone would ping if it picked anything up on the tracking app.

Levon did some stretching exercises to work out the kinks from sleeping on the ground in the chilled damp of the night before. His limbs and joints warmed as the fog lowered to wispy tendrils that moved around the exposed roots of the trees like a silent surf.

He checked the phone and controller. The drone view showed him the haze evaporating in the heat of the rising sun. The shadows of trees fled before the light. Here and there, he could see the rectangles of rooftops set at the base of curved roads as white as lace in the coming day.

A drink of water, a protein bar, and a sliced mango from the marketplace, and he took a seat in a crotch of massive roots at the foot of a spreading kapok. He listened to the forest. A random patter of water fell through the cover of leaves above. The rising and falling twitter and croaking of toads and lizards was giving way to the calls of songbirds.

His phone let out a ping and he snatched up the controller to bring the drone to a halt in its circuit. The ping persisted. He lowered the drone onto a slow course toward the center of the bowl of land. The control screen showed only the green crown of dense foliage. The pings became less frequent. Levon turned the drone first north and then south until the pings grew in regularity and volume. The top of the forest gave way to neat rows of coffee or tea trees that lined the terraces that fell away all the way to the valley floor. Orchards turned to grass until a ribbon of roadway cut across his view. He jinked the drone to follow the road as it turned away to the west and came to an end at a walled compound.

Zooming the camera function in on the compound revealed a half dozen buildings of various sizes around a broad courtyard of either crushed stone or shell. One long building appeared to be a stable or garage. There were no vehicles visible.

There was a rectangular swimming pool of half Olympic length with a pair of buildings set at two sides of one angle. A pool house and guest quarters perhaps. The pool was dry except for a puddle of water at the deep end. Maybe it was being worked on. More likely, it was drained to save on maintenance as the owner was not always in residence.

There were tennis courts behind the pool area. Three courts with green-painted concrete surfaces. A tarp covered a serving machine. The entire section with the courts and pool was surrounded by a high steel fence that segregated it from the rest of the property. A covered walkway led from the pool area to the main house, a large building with several annexes. Like the other structures, it featured gabled roofs of clay tiles. A long greenhouse was set at the rear of a walled courtyard behind the house.

The garage or stable, like the pool area, was joined to the main house by a covered walkway. It was a peculiar feature and Levon wondered at the purpose for it. He wondered as well at the reason for fencing in the pool and tennis areas.

His eyes were drawn to shadows crossing the courtyard. They were converging on a single vector point from all across the property. He dropped the drone to five hundred feet and adjusted his zoom. The shadows were dogs, large dogs. Alsatians, Staffordshires, or mastiffs. They loped toward a pair of men who stopped to snap leashes on them and led them away toward a dog run and kennel building set in the shade of some trees.

He continued watching as the pair of dog handlers moved from the dog run to trot toward the main house. Levon moved the drone to get a view of the rest of the property. He saw a square structure roughly the size of a garden shed sitting isolated against a rear wall of the compound near a back gate.

Following a white strip of road that led from the rear gate brought him to a one-acre clearing at the center of an orchard. It was paved over with a square of concrete and had a steel hangar building set off to one side.

The Leonardo was tied down on the hard stand, tarped over and secured with cables.

His target was likely here. Benny Hung was home.

Levon took one more pass over the property before setting the drone on its return course. He saw new shadows moving away from that tiny blockhouse by the rear gate.

Five animals moving on four legs in a peculiar, spraddled gait. They were elongated and moved at a slow but deliberate pace out into the open courtyard. He knew at first glance they weren't dogs. One of the shapes came to a stop and appeared to lower itself to lie in the sunlight now filling the courtyard.

He focused on the resting shape.

It was a Komodo dragon.

16

Gunny Leffertz said:

"The waiting is what wears on a man."

Levon hiked back down to Bao Loc and took a room at a different hostel. He paid to take a hot shower. He put on a fresh tee and cargo shorts while he waited for his clothes to be cleaned at the laundry. He ate dinner at a stall on a market street while waiting for the clothes to be cleaned and dried. He picked them up, wrapped in newspaper and tied with twine before returning to his room to review the video he took in the morning.

He knew enough about Komodos to know that he wouldn't be entering the compound during daylight hours. The big reptiles looked like they couldn't get out of their own way. That was misleading. They could reach one hundred and fifty pounds in weight and were immensely strong. In addition, they could move at thirty-five miles an hour over short spurts. Their bite was toxic and powerful. Those five could have a man dismembered in seconds.

It explained the sheltered walkways. During the day, the only safe way to move between buildings in the compound was via those conduits. The lizards could not be trained to differentiate between friend and foe. They'd drag down and consume anyone or anything that came within their range.

It would have to be night and the dogs then. And they posed a challenge the dragons didn't. Even if he eluded being attacked, the dogs' barking would alert the compound to his presence.

He was awakened that night by a disturbance outside his room. Loud voices and a woman's scream followed by a man's laughter. Holding the MAB behind his back, Levon slid open his door enough to look into the hall where the hostel's Vietnamese overseer was arguing with a couple in their twenties speaking in Italian.

The man held a rolled-up T-shirt wrapped around one hand. It was bloodstained. Others crowded the hallway to look on and comment. A heavy-set German dressed only in boxers offered to mediate. As it turned out, the Italians unwisely purchased a monkey from a market stall with the intent of turning it into a pet. It bit the man before escaping their room for parts unknown.

"Most likely it took off back to the guy they bought it from, yeah?" an Aussie standing in the door opposite Levon said.

"He's probably sold the same monkey a hundred times," Levon said.

"One monkey looks like another, aye?" the Aussie said, grinning. "You American?"

"Yeah." Levon was using his Dennis Vogel ID here.

"Texas?" the Aussie said hopefully.

"Delaware."

"Don't know where that is," the other shrugged and returned his attention to the drama in the hallway.

Levon slid his door closed and lay back down, falling asleep soon after the noise outside died down.

The next day was spent exploring the area around the Hung compound with a rented motorbike. The monsoon season was coming to an end. The sky was largely clear most of the daylight hours.

Levon used the camera for cover, taking pictures of the landscape, birds, and locals. Workers harvested tea leaves that had fallen to the ground during the rains. They gathered them into baskets which were then dumped into trailers pulled behind trucks.

On the third day, he left the bike hidden under some foliage and climbed the low hill nearest the Hung plantation. He found a place where tall grass grew close to a fringe of trees that covered the crest of the hill. The spot offered him a place of concealment from which he could study the northern face of the compound.

The powerful binoculars brought the buildings and courtyard into reach. Nothing moved including the humped shapes of three of the Komodos down on their haunches in the sun. Over the top of the big house, he could see the tennis courts and a corner of the pool area. The only movement was an automated pool skimmer gliding through the azure water.

He maintained his surveillance through an afternoon drizzle. He came alert when he saw one of the dragons raise itself up on its legs and move at a lazy pace in the direction of the covered walkway that led from the house to the garage. Levon turned his lenses to the walkway and could see a shadow moving on the other side of the cinderblock knee wall topped with a wire fence that protected pedestrians from the lizards.

The Komodo worked up to a swaying lope, following alongside the shadow as it neared the garage. A flash of a glass pane as a man door at the end of the walkway opened. A few seconds later, one of the doors in the bank of garage openings slid upward to allow a white SUV, a 4Runner, out onto the courtyard. The garage closed as the car made its way past the now-halted dragon for the main gate. The steel-grated gateway opened to allow the car out and closed behind it as the 4Runner made its way down the road and out of the holler in the direction of Bao Loc.

It returned a few hours later. Levon had shifted his position for a better view of the walkway and garage. The 4Runner drove into the garage. There was movement under the walkway, a man pushing a wheeled cart. Levon watched him reach the main door which someone had opened from within the garage. Two men emerged after a few moments. One pushed the cart, now loaded with open boxes of what looked like groceries, back toward the house. The other man followed, smoking a cigarette and gesturing as he spoke to his companion.

Levon adjusted his focus to study the men. They were both Asian and both fit and of military age. Both were dressed casually in guayaberas worn open over tank tops. He could see no guns in evidence.

He made a census of the personnel he'd seen so far. There were the two men who'd brought the groceries to the house. They could be servants or bodyguards on double duty. There were also the two dog handlers and supposed dragon wranglers. These men were also Asians, but they appeared to be different men than the two errand runners. That brought his count to four.

The compound was quiet through the afternoon. The rain died away. The sun shone down through a thin veil of overcast. Levon sucked on a tea leaf to stay alert. He stripped off his shirt and rubbed a bug repellent made from eucalyptus on the back of his neck and arms to reduce the clouds of mosquitoes that were starting to rise out of the grass as the sun dropped toward the tops of the ridge that ran along to the west. He smeared some on the sweatband of his Boonie hat.

A peculiar, rhythmic striking sound echoed up from somewhere on the other side of the main house. Levon sent a drone aloft. At a thousand feet, out of earshot and invisible, he guided it toward the source of the sound. It was a repetitious pock, pock, pock coming every two or three seconds.

On his screen he could see a white figure moving back and forth on one of the tennis courts. The serving machine was lobbing Day-Glo yellow balls over the net to be returned again and again by the trotting figure.

Levon adjusted the focus as he zoomed in tighter. It was a slight figure of a male. Impossible to determine age from this angle. The head was covered with a bright red bucket hat. Besides, Viets and Laotians were all of slender builds even into an advanced age.

But from the way the player moved, he decided this was either a boy or a young man. It was none of the four men he'd added to his census earlier.

Possibly a son. Possibly a rentboy staying at the residence for the convenience of the master. None of Levon's research gave him any clue about Hung's sexual proclivities. Articles mentioned a wife and children living in Hanoi but offered little details and no photographs.

The shadows grew long below. The boy tired of his practice and left a litter of dozens of balls on the court. He also left the covering tarp lying by the serving machine as he departed. Further indication that this was a family member or some other privileged house guest rather than a servant wiling away an idle hour.

Levon guided the drone to follow the boy's progress into

the covered walkway that led to the house. He directed the drone away to the skies at his back before entering the command for it to return to him. A pass over the helipad showed him an empty concrete square with a dark oil stain at its center.

The Leonardo was gone. It might be on an errand or it could have taken Hung away.

He continued watching the compound through binoculars for signs of his target. Levon didn't have much hope for that. It explained why the boy was playing alone on the tennis court. An hour or more passed until a movement near the garages caught his eye.

A different garage door rolled up, and a Bobcat trundled out onto the gravel. The driver aimed the shovel end of the little tractor at the nearest dragon. It rose up on its claws and moved away at a brisk trot. The other four were up and walking as well in what appeared to be a learned daily ritual. The Bobcat herded the lizards before it and around the house toward where the dragon hut lay out of sight.

Twenty minutes went by, the sky overhead a rusty orange now. A pair of dogs loped from the house. Levon trained his lenses on them. Staffordshires crossed with mastiffs was his guess. Pitbulls. Dun brown with darker stripes along their flanks. Broadheads with gar mouths lined with fangs. The canine equivalent of a Komodo when properly conditioned.

Satisfied that he'd seen all he could see from his vantage, Levon packed up his gear and hiked back down to where he'd concealed his motorbike. From there, back to his hostel.

He was sitting under party lights in an open-air bar, working on his second beer, when he heard the insect thrum growing overhead. He looked up and spotted the blinking running lights buzzing by overhead.

A yellow Leonardo, nose down and cruising into the depths of the long valley.

It was going to have to be tonight. Levon couldn't risk his target departing for an extended period.

17

Gunny Leffertz said:

"You can go big. You can go small. But you've got to go hard."

The Plantation

THE HALF-MOON WAS a nascent glow through the overcast that blanketed the sky from horizon to horizon. An electric scent was in the air. The rains would begin again soon.

Levon leaped to get a finger grip on the top of the wall. He pulled himself up to swing a leg over and straddle the tiles set in place atop it. He loosened a length of nylon cord he'd tied to his belt to haul up a hemp sack that lay by his backpack lying in the grass at the foot of the wall.

The contents of the sack shifted and chittered as he

lowered it down inside the compound. A yank on the cord undid the loosely knotted drawstring that held the sack closed. Immediately, the pig-tailed monkey scrambled from inside the sack to race across the courtyard. Its paws sprayed gravel in its panic as it ran across the broad open space.

Levon dropped down by his pack to crouch against the wall. He pulled the cording after him. The empty sack remained behind. That couldn't be helped.

Drops fell on his head, making furrows in the grease he'd smeared on his face and the backs of his hands. He dug the Boonie hat from the pocket of his jacket and fit it snugly over his head as the rain fell harder. Over the hiss of the downpour, he could hear barking from the other side of the wall. It grew to a chorus as more and more of the guard dogs gave chase to the intruder.

Barks turned to a continuous baying. The monkey had reached the decorative trees that shaded one side of the house. Outside lights came on around the big house.

Levon shouldered the backpack and ran along the wall until he came to the section that ran behind the garage building. He clambered over the top and dropped into a narrow alley, twenty feet across, that ran between the rear of the garage and the wall.

There was a rear entrance next to a stack of tires covered over with a plastic tarp. It was unlocked. Levon let himself into a storeroom lined with metal shelves stacked with cartons, tools and containers of motor oil. A second door brought him into the garage area.

He flashed the beam of a penlight over the row of vehicles. There was the Bobcat and the Forerunner he'd seen earlier in addition to an H3, a Hilux pickup truck and an older model Porsche two-seater. There were also three custom-painted Yamaha dirt bikes set against the rear wall.

Levon went to work, opening the hood of each car to

slash cables using the K-Bar. He cut the fuel lines on the dirt bikes before slashing the tires of each vehicle.

The sound of the dogs was joined by shouting voices as he exited the back door into the rain. He could see the beams of spotlights stabbing into the sky over the roof of the garage. The drops of rain looked like falling stars in the momentary brilliance.

He was up and over the wall surrounding the compound and moving away from the compound as he heard the first shots. The unmistakable chug of an AK-47. The guns were out now. From the continued sound of three-round bursts and howling dogs, the monkey was making a chase of it.

Levon approached the helipad along a row of tea trees. He left the cover of the trees to run low through tall grass and onto the hard stand until he reached the copter sitting at the center. The rotor and part of the cab was covered over with a tarp that was held in place by steel cables secured to ring bolts set in recesses around the Leonardo.

Lifting one corner of the tarp, he slid open the rear bay door and climbed inside. He laid on his back between the pilot seats and slashed away the wiring under the control console. The helo was disabled for now.

No one was leaving this place anytime soon.

The man door in the broad pull-down door that covered the opening of the hangar was locked. Levon used the butt end of the MAB to knock out one of the plexiglass panes set in the door. It fell inward with a clatter. He reached inside and undid a latch allowing the door to open.

The interior of the hangar was empty except for a long workbench against one wall and a stack of steel drums at the back. He tipped a barrel off the top of the stack and pried off the metal cap. Aviation fuel streamed out with a glugging sound. It created a pool that spread across the concrete.

He set the point of the K-Bar against the skin of the

other barrels and, using the heel of his hand like a mallet, drove wedge-shaped holes through the steel. Fuel came out in a fine spray and the air was rich with the stink of high octane filling the enclosed space.

Levon put a boot to the drum he'd dropped to the floor and launched it rolling toward the hangar door. It rumbled through the growing lake of high octane leaving a tributary behind it before coming to a halt against the door.

Outside, Levon stripped off his jacket, now sodden with fuel, and lit a sleeve with a lighter from the pocket of his khakis. The flames climbed the sleeve greedily. He threw it through the open door into the interior of the hangar.

A rush of heat washed over his back as he ran through the rain from the hangar. For only a second, the area was lit by a flare that brightened the night like noon. He staggered as the concussive wave of expelled air struck him. He only turned back once he'd reached the cover of the grass at the edge of the hardstand.

Thick black smoke belched from the open man door and rose from under the eaves of the roof. The gaps around the hangar door glowed white as though trimmed in wavering neon as the inferno inside grew. The paint on the hangar's exterior was already bubbling and cracking. He could hear a sound like thunder from within as one drum after another reached flashpoint and exploded.

He lay, watching the blaze from within the shelter of the tall grass. He lay low, chin on the ground and the brim of the Boonie hat pulled low. The automatic was in his fist as he watched.

Soon they came. Men with guns. Guns that would be his.

———

THE RAIN STRUCK the skillet hot metal roof causing a

cloud of steam to mingle with the black pall spreading about the burning hangar.

One of the dogs was the first to arrive, racing out of the dark from the compound. It ran, whites around the eyes and yapping, confused by the heat and the smoke. It ran away into the trees. A man appeared in the glow of the fire, calling after it. He had a Kalashnikov slung loose under one arm. He wore a black slicker over his clothes.

A second and third man came from the same direction. One wearing a black T-shirt plastered to his muscular frame. He carried his AK in his fists and scanned the dark around the hangar, head swiveling. The third man was in black slacks and a white dress shirt. He ran ahead to the helicopter and opened the hatch to the cockpit to climb inside.

The pilot.

He must have called the others over because black T-shirt trotted to the helo. Slicker had his back turned, staring in wonder at the swirling tower of embers climbing into the sky. It was paint flakes cooking off and spreading out like slow-motion fireworks.

Levon was up and out of the grass, moving at a run with the stubby MAB held before him in a two-hand grip. He kept the helo between him and the burning building. Reaching the rear fuselage of the Leonardo, he ducked under and came up to see black T-shirt turning toward him, eyes wide. Levon brought him down with a double tap to the chest.

He moved then in a crouch under the tie-down straps. Slicker was turning now, responding to the double bang. Levon shot him on the move. Three rounds to the gut and chest

The pilot was clambering down from the open hatch of the helo, reaching for the AK now trapped under the black

T-shirt's body. Levon shot him twice. The man collapsed against the front landing gear.

The action locked back, Levon tossed aside the small automatic to turn black T-shirt on his back and free the AK. He pulled back the lever to charge it and put a round through black T-shirt's head before putting two more in the pilot. He stepped back from under the tarp. Slicker had managed to lever himself onto his side. Levon put two rounds in his head.

Levon pulled the slicker over what was left of the man's skull before unslinging his rifle. He ejected the magazine and stuck it under the waistband of his khakis. He then pressed down on the release at the back of the bolt cover and threw the bolt and bolt spring away into the dark. He patted the corpse for more ammo and found a fully loaded Taurus revolver in .38 in a holster at the man's side.

He tucked the revolver into his waistband at the small of his back. He plucked a black handheld radio from the man's belt. This he clipped to his own belt after turning the volume to zero.

He did the same with black T-shirt and found no spare magazines. If both magazines were at capacity, he had over fifty rounds plus six in the revolver.

The rain had washed much of the blood and brain matter from the discarded poncho. Levon slipped it over his shoulders and pulled the hood up to cover his head.

At a trot, he moved off the helipad and into the surrounding darkness of the trees.

18

Gunny Leffertz said:
  "When you're in the shit, keep moving."

The Big House

NONE of the men he'd killed were part of his census. Slicker and black T-shirt were bulkier, more athletically built than any of the men he'd previously seen on the compound. These would be two of Benny Hung's personal bodyguards. There would still be the boy, the dog handlers and the errand runners along with Hung and possible guests at the house. Maybe a co-pilot for the helo.

Levon would have preferred a complete census except there was no way of knowing how long Hung would be visiting. It might be weeks before he returned again. He was committed now. It was mission go.

The sound of the pouring rain combined with the roar of the fuel fire had probably masked the gunfire at the helipad from anyone in the house. Even if they heard it, it would have been the familiar chug of a Kalashnikov. They would assume the bodyguards were taking care of an intruder.

He trotted through trees along a path that roughly followed the trail from the walled compound to the hangar area. A man leading a dog on a leash was approaching from the open gate. The dog was pulling the other man, the lead line taut.

Levon stepped from cover. The man turned to him, a hand raised in greeting. The dog's ears were back, head canted.

He shot the dog first. The man second. Two rounds center mass for each. He put slugs in each of their heads before crouching to remove the magazine from the AK the dog handler had slung over his back.

He had close to ninety rounds now. Four dead and only one from his original count.

The compound was lit like a night game. Using the gate for his approach was out of the question. The slicker would not hold up as a disguise for a prolonged time. It would not conceal his height.

Levon moved back along the section of wall that ran behind the garages. He was up and over and running along the alley that ran across the rear of the garage building.

A turkey peek around the end of the building. No one was moving in the misty light cast down from the banks of lights under the eaves of the house. No men. No dogs.

He checked the radio on his belt. The indicator light was not flashing. No one was transmitting. He took that as a positive.

All eyes would be turned to the north toward the flames rising over the treetops. Levon walked rather than ran across the open space between the end of the garages and a clutch of bamboo set against the southern wall. Running was a giveaway. If anyone saw a man walking they would assume it was someone who belonged there.

He kept the bamboo between him and the house until the growth came to an end fifty feet shy of the main gate. At a casual gait, he followed the drive to a walkway of concrete blocks set in gravel that led toward the big house. He was not challenged. This led him along the south wall and around to the rear of the house. The windows overhead were all dark. Rainwater gurgled in the downspouts from gutters two stories above.

At the rear of the house, a waist-high fence of wrought iron surrounded a cellar entrance. Reflected light from rooms deeper in the house shone against the windows of the kitchen wing above. The gate on the wrought-iron fence was crusted with rust under cracked black enamel. He stepped over the fence rather than risk the squeal of protesting hinges. Ten steps carried him down to a niche set at the base of the kitchen wall.

Levon tried the latch on the door, and it gave. He was inside a dark room that smelled of garlic and spoiled cabbage. He shut the door behind him, and the ambient hiss of rainfall was replaced with near silence. There were faint footfalls to be heard from above. He could not hear voices. The ceiling above was concrete and would be tiled above. He allowed himself a few moments with his eyes shut to accustom himself to the dark.

It was a cool place with stone walls and spaced with brick support columns. There were crates stacked against one wall. A pair of chest freezers hummed against one another. An archway led to the dead end of a wine cellar, rows of dusty bottles on wooden racks. Another dead end was a utility room with a damp floor where a pair of air handlers vibrated.

A narrow corridor brought him to a wooden staircase that led to a landing above. He moved to the top; the rifle held tight to his side. A thin blade of yellow light could be seen in the gap along the floor. No shadows disturbed it. He pressed his ear to the door and heard nothing from the other side.

Levon stood a while listening, his eyes on the bar of light cast on his feet, watching for movement. A rumble of voices rose in volume from somewhere within. From the echoes, it sounded to be several rooms away from whatever space the door opened into. The voices were muffled but one rose above the others either asking questions or giving commands.

The green indicator light on the radio was blinking. Someone was transmitting, trying to reach the team that had gone down to the helipad to secure the Leonardo.

Staying low, the AK held close at his side, he tested the knob. It turned. He opened the door a crack. The voices became clearer but no closer. He inched the door wider to find it opened into a pantry room lined with shelves stacked with cans and jars. Wooden bins held onions and yams and potatoes. The room was dark, illuminated only by light coming in through an open door at the far end of the room.

There was a butcher table above which was set a magnetic strip of cleavers and carving knives. Levon chose a long-bladed carving knife with blade and handle forged from a single piece of steel. This he slipped under his belt on his left side.

He took up a position just inside the doorway. The shouting voice was clearer now but receding into another room. He could make out words though he couldn't understand them. The voice was male and spoke with an unquestioned authority.

From his place by the door, he could see a large kitchen area. Decorative cabinets, a commercial stove and a bank of ovens. The room was lit indirectly by lights wired under the cabinets above a steel countertop.

Levon stripped off the slicker and moved into the room and across the tile floor. He moved at a half crouch so as not to be visible from the outside through the row of windows that faced the back of the compound. He had the AK up to his shoulder and sighted along the barrel as he reached a broad open entryway that led into the more brightly lit interior of the house.

He halted as a shadow fell across the tiles from the entryway. It grew in breadth and length. Levon slid the carving knife from his belt.

A man entered at an easy walk. One of the errand runners. The man was unarmed and moving at an easy gait toward a pair of Subzero refrigerators set into a wall.

Levon caught the man as he pulled open one of the doors of the fridge but before he could reach for one of the beers lining a shelf within. He took the man in a chokehold, yanked him away from the glow of the open door and backward into the pantry.

The point of the carving knife slid between the vertebrae at the base of the struggling man's skull. The body went limp, and Levon dropped it to the floor. He left the blade lodged in the bone and made his way from the pantry and back into the kitchen.

Rifle up, he passed into a formal dining area and past a long table covered in a cloth and a row of chairs stacked upon one another. A broad archway at the far end led into an entry foyer open to the second floor and lined with marble columns. A granite floored stairway led to the upper levels.

The brittle squelch of a radio caused Levon to turn to where a man stepped from between two columns. The other errand runner. Two rounds dropped him to the floor. The double boom of the rifle echoed through the house. A frantic voice rose crackling from the radio on the dead man's belt.

Levon stooped to turn the dead man's radio volume up. He could hear the same voice from the radio continuing faintly from upstairs. He charged up to the first landing taking two steps at a time. The radio went hush below him. Above him, the space went silent.

Transversing his sight view from left to right, he covered the balcony above as he moved up at a more deliberate pace for the next floor. A turkey peek around a corner at the top of the stairs resulted in a long spray of automatic fire that tore up the carpeted floor and misted the air with plaster dust.

Levon dropped to his side to return suppression fire in a three-round burst. A figure ducked back behind a door that opened into a paneled hallway lined with framed artwork. His next burst went through the door. A rifle clattered to the floor from behind the door. A figure collapsed against the door spilling it wide. The second dog handler.

Levon moved forward down the center of the hall. As he neared the fallen man, he saw the loop of a dog lead around the man's wrist.

The creature exploded from the room, paws scrabbling on carpet. It turned to launch itself at Levon, the arc of its leap carrying it under the barrel of his AK. Rather than strike him bodily, the Doberman gnashed at his left arm. It caught mostly cloth but managed to sink a few teeth into the flesh of his forearm. The dog's weight was pulling him off balance. He released the rifle to fall to the floor. He pulled the Taurus from the waistband at his back just as a man following the dog from the room raised a shotgun at him.

Levon snapped off a shot from the revolver that took the man high in the chest. The man, an unknown not in the census, stumbled back, the shotgun discharging into the ceiling. Plaster rained down. Levon pressed the revolver into the dog's ribs and pulled the trigger twice. The animal fell away, its legs kicking. Two more .38s into the chest of the fallen man, a gray-haired Asian in a flowered shirt. The shotgun was an elaborately engraved double barrel with checkered stock. A gaming piece.

Dropping the revolver to the floor, he snatched up the AK once more. Blood was soaking into his shirt sleeve, running to the floor in a stream. There was nothing to be done about that now. He moved toward the open doorway, stepping over the body of the gray-haired man. The man had one of the radios on his belt. A querulous male voice came tinny from the speaker.

Levon unclipped the radio on his belt after exchanging magazines in the AK. He pressed the respond button twice. The voice became more insistent, demanding. He squelched twice more before moving into the room the two men and the dog had exited. The radio went silent.

The room was a bedroom. Spacious with a king-size bed atop a pedestal beneath a ceiling of decorative plaster. Mirrors were framed by a filigree carved or molded with roses and vines painted white to look like icing on a cake. Heavy teak furniture lined the walls of either a colonial vintage or some kind of recreation. An enormous painting of a naked man embracing a naked woman on a rocky escarpment beneath a stormy sky hung above the bed. It was in a thick gilded frame and looked like something off the covers of the paperbacks his mom used to read.

Beyond the bed, a full-length mirror in a frame to match the painting stood away from the wall at an angle. Levon stepped to one side and raised the rifle at the glass. He could see his image there. His features dark with grease. The sleeve of his left arm black with blood. His face a mask.

He depressed the respond tab and heard an answering squelch from behind the mirror. No voice rose to answer.

He fired three rounds toward the mirror. The slugs punched holes through the glass, starring it. Each round made a ringing sound as though they'd struck metal.

Levon launched himself forward then. The mirror was being drawn back toward the wall by someone inside. Before it could close entirely, he jammed the end of the Kalashnikov into the gap. He pulled the trigger spraying a long burst into the room.

A keening sound came from within. An animal cry. Levon shouldered the door wider allowing him to turn the rifle in a wider arc for another burst. He pressed it open to enter the room in a crouch.

Benny Hung was on the floor, clawing at the tile to drag himself away from the door. An automatic lay out of reach. He was dressed in a robe and some kind of silk pajama bottoms now sodden with his blood. The burst from the AK had caught him in the thighs and lower abdomen. The man was bleeding out.

He turned his head, gasping, the whites of his eyes showing all around. He stared at the man looming closer, pale unblinking eyes watching him over the ring sight.

Levon put three rounds into the feebly crawling man on the floor. One through his chest. Two more turned his skull to a wet, broken vessel.

The room was windowless with unadorned walls of poured concrete slabs. A standing vault stood open. On one side, a row of rifles and shotguns, hunting pieces standing upright in a rack. On the other were steel drawers. Set below was a shelf upon which there was a heap of cases for jewelry and watches. Framed canvasses leaned against another wall. To Levon's untrained eye, they looked like more valuable, more serious works of art than the tacky masterpiece that hung above the bed.

Levon turned to the open doorway, rifle raised to the room beyond. The mirror outside hid a heavy steel door fitted with a triple set of bar locks. This was Hung's final refuge, a panic room as well as his treasure vault.

He'd come back to this. For now, he had more urgent matters. His arm was still bleeding. And he was still in the house of the enemy. He squawked the radio but received no reply. It could be all the bodyguards were already taken care of. Or it could mean the remaining ones were playing it smart. His rough census was checked off. Complete as far as he knew. But there was always a wild card.

Levon pulled the bullet-riddled bedroom door shut then shouldered a heavy armoire across it as a barricade.

In the spa-like bathroom off the master suite, he pulled off his shirt before using his belt as a tourniquet around his left bicep. The bleeding slowed; he washed the wound under a golden tap. Most of the brand names in the medicine cabinet were unknown to him. He picked one that looked like an astringent and poured the entire bottle over the bite. It burned like fire and that was good. He'd need stitches but that could wait.

He was in the process of covering the wound with a dressing of clean toweling. A shift in light caused him to turn, a movement in the reflection of a bronzed mirrored wall.

He snatched at the end of a rifle barrel being used to push the bathroom door open. Levon yanked the rifle toward him at the same driving the bearer onto the point of the K-Bar gripped in his fist. He slammed the dagger hard into the soft tissue of the gunman, pulling the man close to him as the point angled up beneath the ribs.

It wasn't a man.

It was the boy he'd seen on the tennis court. Wide eyes, rimmed black with streaks of kohl, stared up into his. They turned glassy, unseeing. The boy was naked but for a pair of silk board shorts. He was young. Still an adolescent. A hand clawed weakly at Levon's wounded arm. Levon shoved the blade harder, turning it. The hand fell away to swing limp. The eyes turned to dull onyx.

Levon let him slide to the tiles before scanning the empty bedroom. The armoire barricade was still in place. The boy had been hiding in the room the entire time. The rifle that lay on the floor, a vintage Mannlicher bolt action, had been retrieved from the vault in the panic room.

The wound on his arm was bleeding freely now. Levon repeated the process of cleaning and disinfecting it before securing a towel tight about his forearm with a sash cord torn from the bedroom drapes. His T-shirt was plastered to him with a mix of his own and the boy's blood. He stripped it off and tossed it in a standing soaking tub. His khakis were soaked with blood as well but there was little to be done about that now.

His injury bound, he recharged the AK with his last magazine and returned to the bedroom. There, he re-entered the panic room and helped himself to several boxes of 7.62 for the rifle as well as three fat wads of cash taken from one of the drawers. He stuffed these, a bundle of Thai bahts, one of Malaysian ringgits and another of American hundreds, into the cargo pockets of his khakis.

He tried squelching the radio again. Still no response.

Levon killed the lights in the room and waited, eyes closed, in the dark for a count of one hundred and twenty. He parted the drapes and pulled open a pair of French doors that led onto a broad terrace that ran across the rear face of the house and into the glare of the bright lights arrayed under the eaves. The light was diffused by the heavy downpour now lashing the house.

Staying close to the wall and the remaining shadows, he found the steps leading down to a kind of veranda and from there the main grounds. Moving from one collection of shadows to the next, he reached a pair of thousand-gallon propane tanks. He turned the cocks on each to closed.

Somewhere, the faint chugging of a generator died away and the lights about the house went dark.

He crouched in the rain, listening and waiting and watching the area around the propane tanks.

After he waited an hour, no one had come. No dogs. No men.

Still wary, he moved through the dark for the rear gate, passing by the blockhouse in which the Komodos slept. Fuel still burned inside the hangar but the fire was now only a red glow barely visible through the pall of choking smoke hovering over the helipad area.

He entered the trees beyond the hardstand and retrieved his backpack. His boots, khakis, and socks came off to be set aside. He slid on fresh cargo shorts, socks, T-shirt, and wool pullover. The khakis he balled up and stuffed into the ruck before shouldering it. The AK slung ready from his arm, he hiked deeper into the trees toward the place where the green hills met and he knew a game trail would take him out of the valley where he would turn west.

He hurt, both from the exertion of the night and the throbbing ache of the dog bite. Still, he felt a new strength in his legs as he walked. It was as though a weight had been lifted from him. It gifted him with new vigor even as the adrenaline of the fight leeched vigor from his limbs. It was replaced by the buoyant feeling that always came with survival, the sweet sensation that comes with walking away from a battle.

But he knew it would pass. It always did. And when the new strength was gone he'd still have to keep moving to put miles between him and the men he'd left behind. He'd need to keep that pace for days, even weeks, as he followed trails westward, staying to the forest, fording rivers only by night.

19

Gunny Leffertz said:

"The forest is a supermarket if you know where to look."

Bangkok

TWO WEEKS WALKING TOOK him across Cambodia to the Thai border. The first leg was five days of hiking over one mountain and across one valley after another. He avoided contact with the remote villages and stayed off of roadways. He lived wild, eating cardamom, wild peppers, and bamboo. He snared rabbits and killed a small deer. He boiled his drinking water in a small pot he'd packed. The nights in the hills were colder than he'd anticipated. He buried his cook-fire in a layer of earth and slept atop the embers.

After burying the AK and ammo, Levon descended the highlands to follow an established hiking trail that carried him west in the company of parties of adventure tourists from Spain and Austria and Norway. He was Canadian Tom Creighton again hiking from hostel to hostel on sabbatical from the University of Toronto.

Twenty pounds lighter, his clothing stiff with sweat and dust, his boots worn flat, he crossed into Thailand at Ban Pakkad. He told the border guards there that he was on a day trip to the farm market at Tambon Khlong Yai. Once there, he paid to have his clothes laundered and took a long, steaming shower. Roadworn but cleaned up, he joined a mixed group of tourists from New Zealand and Ireland and rode a bus with them to a place called Thap Sai. From there, he paid passage on a sleeper bus to Bangkok.

At the Qatar Airlines desk at Suvarnabhumi Airport he was told that he would need a travel visa from the Canadian consulate as his last entry stamp was from his arrival in Ho Chi Minh City. There was also the matter of him paying in cash. He was asked to wait in their traveler's lounge while the consulate was notified.

Levon helped himself to coffee and French pastries and took a seat to watch planes landing and taking off. After a while, he fell into a deep sleep.

Someone prodded his boot with the toe of a polished patent leather pump. Levon looked up to see a petite woman in eyeglasses and black pantsuit smiling at him. Standing behind her was a trio of US Marines who were not smiling.

"Leslie Stuckey, sir. I'm with the State Department."

"Which state department?" But Levon already knew.

"The United States State Department, Mr. Cade."

20

Gunny Leffertz said:

"The fella who said 'It's better to apologize than seek permission' must have never really fucked up."

Andersen Air Force Base, Guam

TWO SKY COPS came to escort Levon from the guardhouse before dawn. They ordered him to back up to the cell door and stick his hands through the slot to be flex-cuffed. The two hungover airmen sharing the cell slurred farewells as he was hauled away. The pair of MPs marched him by a row of Blackhawks tied down to hardstands on the opposite side of a razor wire topped fence. The sun was a pink glow on the horizon but already the air felt like the inside of a sauna. He was running with sweat under the jumpsuit of faded blue they'd given him two days prior. His feet slapped on the asphalt walkway, the soles of his slip-on tennis shoes squeaking.

They put him in the rear seat of a Humvee and belted him in securely. One MP took the rear passenger seat next to him while the other drove. They left the guardhouse compound to drive along a four-lane ring road divided by a manicured median strip. They were waved past a gate and pulled up to a steel-walled admin building with the symbol for the 36th Wing PACAF, "Prepared to Prevail" on a sign by the entrance walkway.

The interior of the building felt like a walk-in freezer after the heat outside. The sky cops showed papers to a sergeant at a desk who waved over an airman first class to show them along a corridor lined with office doors. The airman was a busty redhead who eyed him with open suspicion.

At the end of the hall, the red-headed airman knocked at a door and was told to enter. She held the door for the MPs who shoved Levon into the room.

A sanguine-looking man sat at a table in what appeared to be a secured conference room. No windows. No cameras. Not even an electrical outlet in the walls. The table before him was empty of papers or devices. Only a foam coffee cup rested by his hand. The man was perhaps in his forties or a very fit fifties. He wore a light sport coat over a black polo shirt. His resting expression was bland disinterest.

One of the sky cops offered paperwork that the man waved away.

"Please cut those cuffs off him," the man said.

"Sir, our orders were—" a sky cop began.

"And I'm changing those orders," the man said without rancor, without a raised voice.

"Sir." The sky cop used a clasp knife to sever the plastic band and Levon's hands were free.

"Have you had breakfast?" the man said, gesturing for Levon to take a seat opposite him.

"No."

"I'm afraid all I can offer is coffee," the man said, looking to the redhead still at the door by the sky cops. Her frown of suspicion turned to a scowl before she turned to her new errand.

"Sir, will you require us to stay?" the lead sky cop, a corporal, said.

"I don't think Mr. Cade will get frisky," the man said, cocking an eyebrow at Levon. "But if you could stay handy, I'd appreciate it."

"Will we be escorting the prisoner back to the guardhouse?"

"That will be entirely up to Mr. Cade."

The redhead returned with a foam cup of coffee, a stirrer, sugars, and two creams. She set them down before Levon before departing with the MPs. The door closed behind them.

"Oh, I bet *your* ears have been burning," the man said, sitting back in his chair.

"What agency are you with?" Levon asked as he poured three packs of sugar into his cup. "You're not bureau, or you'd have flashed ID already."

"Let's not bother with details." The man spoke in a clipped, private school accent but Levon detected a bit of a drawl. A southern boy turned Yankee.

"What makes me rate this kind of attention? I knew I was in deep shit, only not *this* deep."

"Oh, it is *deep*, and it is *wide*, Mr. Cade. You have fucked up so big that we might run out of letters in the alphabet before we run out of agencies that want your ass. Both foreign and domestic. I think State is ready to add a deputy secretary tasked solely with making the rest of your life as miserable as possible."

Levon shrugged.

"But then there is the broader picture," the man said, thin lips pressing back a smile. "There is the question of who benefits. What practical purpose is served with pilloring someone like you?"

"Like me."

"One of our country's unsung heroes. One of Orwell's 'rough men.' Are you familiar with the quote?"

Levon nodded as he took a sip of the lukewarm coffee.

"After all, what harm have you done? Well, obviously, quite a *bit* of harm to certain individuals and entities. And, as it turns out, each of these individuals and entities are, were, of interest to your government."

"Are you some kind of wizard?" Levon asked abruptly. "Or did they send you here to fuck with me?"

"Excuse me?"

"Are you here to magic my ass out of the clusterfuck I created? Or maybe you just like to hear yourself talk."

"Mr. Cade, a man in your desperate situation—"

"Sir, I am so past desperation I can't even remember what that feels like. I did what I did, and I have no regrets. If you know so much about me, you know why I did it. And if you think you can use that against me for some dark purpose of your own, then you can fuck yourself. I've run my string out. I'm done with what I came to do."

"For your daughters," the man said after a moment, his voice lowered.

Levon fixed him with a hard stare.

"Yes, we know about them. And, no, we don't know where they are. You taught them well. They remain hidden or beyond our grasp. I could lie to you. I could say we had them in custody to apply pressure to you. But that's not what I'm here for."

"You're not lying to me. You're not playing with me. You're not sitting there with that shit-eating grin telling me there's a way out for me." There was accusation in Levon's tone. He was expressing his deepest distrust of this nameless man from nowhere.

"You could go home. Back to your girls. Your farm. Your own name."

"My farm."

"I'm told the grass has grown back over the grave sites."

"You can clear that. You can make that all right with the law."

Now it was the man in the polo shirt's turn to shrug.

"Look, you've been in the belly of the beast, Mr. Cade. You know as well as I do there is no rule of law anymore. Good and bad, legal and illegal, are what we *say* they are given the situation. What we do is weigh the benefits and the harm, the profits and losses."

"And where do I come out on the balance sheet?"

"To the good, Mr. Cade. Or at least even. Though your methods are more direct than we would prefer, your actions in the past few weeks have presented certain opportunities that were not previously available to us. You have not only eliminated top figures in two international cartels, but you have set them against one another, each laying the blame for your actions at the other's doorstep."

Levon remembered Benny Hung's guest, the gray-haired man in the flowered shirt.

"This change in the order at the top of the Red House leaves a vacuum. One we can readily fill with an actor of our own. The Red House is typical of Asian gangs with its ties into politics, military, and business. Your disruption in the status quo has offered us an opportunity, a hand to play in an area we've been anxious to participate in."

"And what are you asking *me* to do?"

"Nothing." The man spread his hands. "You do nothing at all. We know from your history that you can be trusted.

Or rather, we know you will mind your own business so long as we mind ours."

"I just go back home and all's forgiven. Like that shit in Idaho and Alabama never happened."

"Or Mexico." The man struggled to suppress a smile this time.

"So, do I sign something or swear on a Bible or what?"

"Mr. Cade, now who's fucking with who?" the man said with an open grin.

Gunny Leffertz said:
"The trouble isn't gettin' home. It's bein' *home."*

Alabama

EXCEPT FOR THE faded ribbons of police tape, everything looked much as they'd left it. The house, stable and the steel shed lay open to the elements. The house smelled rank of urine and skat where coyotes or wild dogs had used it as a lair. That kept Rascal, the Jack Russell, busy sniffing every corner. Bella, the aging bluetick hound, took up her usual spot, curling up on the porch between the wicker-backed rockers.

There was trash everywhere from the thorough search law enforcement had put the house through. Floorboards were pulled up and some plaster and lathe torn from the studs. Anything they'd left behind in drawers or closets was scattered on the floor. About the only thing they didn't touch was the rows of old paperbacks in the bookcase in the living room.

Merry gave her uncle a list of cleaning supplies they'd need. Fern left the girls to start the clean-up, driving the Dodge truck with Michigan plates over to the Walmart in Haley. He promised to bring back some Wendy's too.

They started by tearing down all the tape. It looked like the sad remnants of some holiday long past. The electricity was dead, but there was enough water in the captive air tank to give them a start on the kitchen floor where most of the coyote piss and shit was. They swept up what they could.

There was a half-full gallon bottle of ammonia left under the sink. They opened all the windows and diluted the stuff in a bucket of water. Hope poured enough to wet the floor while Merry scrubbed away with a sponge mop until the worst of the odor was gone. Uncle Fern would most likely have to tear up the linoleum and underflooring to get rid of it all.

The girls left the house to allow the sharp ammonia stink to evaporate. Hope took a seat in one of the rockers. Rascal immediately jumped into her lap, nuzzling at her hand to be petted. Merry set a Winchester lever action down atop the wobbly cane table by the other chair.

"Will we need that?" Hope said, idly scratching the terrier behind the ears.

"Maybe." Merry shrugged, pulling rubber cleaning gloves off her hands. "The coyotes might come back."

"Uncle Fern says there will be no more trouble," Hope said.

"He doesn't like to worry us."

"Uncle Fern said all the men who might hurt us are gone."

"He can't know that for sure, Hopey."

"When will we know for sure?"

Merry was formulating an answer to that imponderable when she heard tires crushing gravel. Somewhere beyond the trees, where the long driveway turned from the county road, a vehicle was approaching. Yellow dust rose through the treetops. It was too soon for their uncle to be returning.

Rascal heard the sound as well and launched himself from Hope's lap. He bounded down the drive toward the sound, yapping as his paws left the ground in his peculiar leaping gait. Merry laid a hand on the rifle, eyes locked on the pall of dust moving toward the house through the branches. Hope turned to her, eyes wary until she saw a broad smile crease her big sister's face.

A truck, a battered old Chevy Silverado shot with primer, was coming up toward the stable yard pulling behind it a brand new, two-tone Sundowner horse trailer. A hand waved to them from the open window of the truck's cab.

Merry was off the porch first, the rifle forgotten, with Hope close behind as they raced to catch up with the dog now pelting hard alongside the truck and trailer.

TAKE A LOOK AT: DROWNING ARE THE DEAD

BY BRENT TOWNS

BEST-SELLING AUTHOR BRENT TOWNS RETURNS WITH THIS PRIVATE DETECTIVE MYSTERY—FULL OF SMALL-TOWN SECRECY AND DEADLY INTRIGUE.

In the middle of Australia's Outback lies the small town of Friar's Lake. It's quaint, quiet, and—more importantly—devoid of crime.

So, when a body turns up with the hallmark signs of a manic serial killer from the past, Private Investigator Trent Jacobs is hired by a town local to find out if Ten Cent—the infamous killer—is back.

But as this once-quiet town begins to unravel, tragedy strikes again, and Trent goes missing.

Thankfully, newcomer Mark Hayes is eager to help out. Until—with every shocking secret that's uncovered, he begins to question whether he can find the killer before time runs out.

After all...beneath small-town Friar Lake's dusty exterior, there are hidden truths of which even the locals are unaware.

AVAILABLE NOW

ABOUT THE AUTHOR

Born and raised in Philadelphia, Chuck Dixon worked a variety of jobs from driving an ice cream truck to working graveyard at a 7-11 before trying his hand as a writer. After a brief sojourn in children's books he turned to his childhood love of comic books. In his thirty years as a writer for Marvel, DC Comics and other publishers, Chuck built a reputation as a prolific and versatile freelancer working on a wide variety titles and genres from Conan the Barbarian to SpongeBob SquarePants. His graphic novel adaptation of J.R.R. Tolkien's *The Hobbit* continues to be an international bestseller translated into fifty languages. He is the co-creator (with Graham Nolan) of the Batman villain Bane, the first enduring member added to the Dark Knight's rogue's gallery in forty years. He was also one of the seminal writers responsible for the continuing popularity of Marvel Comics' The Punisher.

After making his name in comics, Chuck moved to prose in 2011 and has since written over twenty novels, mostly in the action-thriller genre with a few side-trips to horror, hardboiled noir and western. The transition from the comics form to prose has been a life-altering event for him. As Chuck says, *"writing a comic is like getting on a roller coaster while writing a novel is more like a long car trip with a bunch of people you'll learn to hate."* His Levon Cade novels are currently in production as a television series from Sylvester Stallone's Balboa Productions. He currently lives in central Florida and, no, he does not miss the snow.